C@UGHT IN THE WEB

OTHER WORKS BY PETER DIXON

FICTION
TR@HISON (France)
Hunting the Dragon
Coulez le Lucky Dragon (France)
The Olympian
Operation Bluewater (France)
The True Love
The Children are Watching (with Laird Koenig)

FOR YOUNGER READERS
The Young Adventurers (six action adventure novels)
Sealab 2020
The Homesteaders

NONFICTION
The Complete Guide to Surfing
Le Guide Complete du Surf
Vasectomy Sex and Parenthood (with Norman Fleishman)
Children, Families and the Sea (five books with Sarah Dixon)
West Coast Beaches (with Sarah Dixon)
Hang Gliding
Hot Skateboarding (with Pahl Dixon)
Ballooning
Soaring
The Silent Adventure
Men Who Ride Mountains
Where the Surfers Are
Men and Waves
The Complete Book of Surfing

First published in France by Éditions Yago 2011

Copyright Peter Dixon 2013

ISBN 978-0615739243

Cover Design by Laurie Thinot

Edited by Sarah Dixon

Garamond
Century Gothic
Papyrus

Published by
Octagon Productions, Inc.
PO Box 6235
Malibu, California 90264-6235
U.S.A.

Peter Dixon

C@UGHT IN THE WEB

A NOVEL

AN OCTAGON BOOK

To Laird Koenig

*Who embarked with me on a
writer's long voyage of hard work
and friendship*

AND SO IT BEGAN...

In the dimness of a summer cabin hard rain beating on a cedar shake roof gave a steady accompaniment to the frenzied clicking of a computer keyboard. A young man with swimmer's wide muscular shoulders — but if we looked more closely he wasn't all that young — sat upright at a knocked together desk. His eyes were intently focused on the glowing screen. The bluish electronic glow illuminated an advanced assemblage of multi mega gigabyte hard drives, a video game joystick, and printer-scanner.

Rapid breathing added to the chaotic angry energy the hacker projected as he rapidly manipulated mouse, keyboard, and gamer's joystick. His shadowy face was fixed upon the computer screen and a skillfully animated do-it-yourself shooter video game. On the screen two figures confronted one another. Only their faces had been given identifiable characteristics. The photo realistic background was the hard slum street of a mean city. The shooter pointed an oversize handgun at his victim who slowly raised his arms in surrender. The hacker's manic panting and seething murmurs grew increasingly louder. Releasing years of pent up hostility he hissed manically, "Die you bastard!"

The surrendering stick figure knew he faced a hardened killer. Attempting to escape, he spun and sprinted down a dark trash strewn alley. The young man's fingers supplied sounds of running feet and then he voiced two abrupt gunshots. POW! POW! The animated bullet struck the fleeing man, blood erupted from his shattered skull, and he died on the filthy pavement.

"Got you Greenlee. Now I get back what's mine."

CHAPTER ONE

From an altitude of twenty-five hundred feet the floatplane pilot studied the wind-ruffled water around Alex Greenlee's four square mile island. He would be landing there in a few minutes and a little chop on the surface would help the pontoons break free on takeoff. He'd have no trouble departing today. He liked putting down at the family's private, deep water inlet. There were no boats or other aircraft tied up to the long wooden dock except for Greenlee's immaculate sloop and the old caretaker's weathered sailing dory.

The pilot was a few minutes ahead of schedule and he banked the old blue and white Canadian-built bush plane to circle the densely forested island. Unlike dozens of other islands in Washington's San Juans, this one showed no scars from clear-cut logging, road building and summer housing developments. Except for the large stone and timber estate that Alex Greenlee had built two-hundred feet inland from the dock, the pilot imagined the island looked much the same as when it emerged from the last ice age.

Off the island's northwest headland the pilot spotted an eruption of misty vapor spouting from the blow hole of a surfacing killer whale. From his altitude he counted seven more in the orca pod. He knew they liked to patrol the shallow water off the headland where sea lions and salmon were easy prey.

A small lake near the center of the island dazzled sun into his eyes. He'd heard that a few wild Chinook salmon still spawned up the narrow, swift-flowing stream that drained from the lake into the Strait of Juan de Fuca.

There were not many wild Chinook left among the San Juans. Those that had survived nets, hooks, and pollution were genetically altered by breeding with escaped farm-raised salmon. He thought about asking Mr. Greenlee for permission to fish the lake, but he knew he'd be refused. The pilot liked Alex Greenlee. After three years of flying him back and forth between the island estate and Seattle, he understood the intense man's fierce defense of his island sanctuary. If he had even a small part of Greenlee's millions he'd want privacy too.

The pilot reached for binoculars and glassed the inlet. Mr. and Mrs. Greenlee were on their way to the dock. The younger woman, whom he'd flown in two days ago, followed them. Where was their son? The shy boy, who hardly ever left the island, usually met the plane to ask for the mail. He shifted the binoculars to scan the main house. In an open upstairs window he saw the glow of a computer screen. The boy was at it again. The pilot glanced at his watch. He was still early. He would make one more pass around the island and then land.

14

What the pilot could not see through the open upstairs window of the Greenlee house was a sandy haired, overweight eleven-year-old boy sprawled on a leather couch reading an e-mail on his 42-inch computer monitor mounted on the wall over his desk. The boy, at that moment, was totally focused on the message he had received over the Internet only moments ago.

> Hi there, Simon,
> Thanks for your order. My personally autographed wrestling action poster, inscribed to you, went out snail mail last week. Don't forget to watch my big grudge match with "Killer Kane" on the 29th. Guess who's going to do the killing?
> Your Cyberspace Pal, Crusher

The boy calculated that the poster of the wrestler and his new computer game would arrive with the groceries on the chartered floatplane that was now landing to fly his mother and father to Seattle. He suspected that Crusher's note was a blanket acknowledgment to all the wrestler's fans who had ordered the full color photo over the Internet. That was okay with Simon. At least someone out there in cyberspace had, electronically or not, acknowledged that he was a Crusher fan. Professional television wrestling, with its classic violent drama of good guys fighting bad, had hooked the boy with the same intensity as he had embraced the Internet and video games.

Simon understood that pro wrestlers were really steroid augmented athletic actors faking their staged mortal combat. Even so, he found the colorful theatrics and bombastic violence of the players as real as his isolated existence on the Greenlee family island.

He thought about sending Crusher a thank you e-mail, but decided to wait until the poster actually arrived. His father had told him often enough that in business dealings one should never appear overly eager or the competition would sense weakness and use it to their advantage.

Simon looked up from his wireless keyboard and mouse that rested on the coffee table in front of the couch. He glanced at the honey blonde Port Orford cedar paneling to the left of his desk. He decided he'd Scotch tape Crusher's poster there. His father had warned that the tall straight grain mostly knot-free Oregon cedars were an endangered tree and had been almost logged to extinction. With unusual firmness, Simon was forbidden from driving nails, pins, or even staples into the rare wood. For some reason that the boy couldn't understand, his father had a reverence for trees and the wood they provided.

"If Crusher didn't rip me off it'll be on the plane," Simon thought. He had used his father's business credit card number to pay for the poster, the new BAD WORLD computer game he was expecting, and dozens of others he had ordered over the last two years. His dad would never know because the boy had secretly accessed Alex Greenlee's computer mainframe and hacked Greenlee Electronics' business account number.

He could have taken the credit card from his dad's wallet to obtain the number, but to Simon that would be stealing. He was careful not to overdo his Internet use of the card. So far, Greenlee's accountancy firm had not questioned the two-to-three hundred dollars a month plus handling and postage paid electronically to his favorite on line computer gaming store and the CrusherCorp charge of nineteen-ninety-five plus postage and handling.

A deft left-handed movement of the mouse deleted the Crusher's e-mail and Simon surfed the net searching for a favorite website.

The boy quickly found a computer game chat room and read the ongoing back and forth critique of a real-time 3-D gangster-shooter game titled, Ghetto Blaster: Life of Crime. One of the Internet players found the violent and challenging game 'cool', especially the choice of weapons used to escape the crime-ridden ghetto where the action took place. Low life adversaries could be attacked with pipes and clubs, pistols, automatic rifles and even flame throwers. Simon thought of logging on to the Ghetto Blaster web site and trying a preview of the game. He hesitated, knowing that if he began to play, he'd become hooked and would have to order it.

With every computer in the house linked to his father's new five hundred terabyte mainframe, he opted for caution. As he had been told again and again, "You never know who is going to be reading your e-mails."

Alex's latest anti-spy ware security program hadn't stopped Simon. He knew that if he could break in so could hackers from the outside. Simon reasoned that since no one knew his father's private at home computer password but his dad and himself, that secret was safe.

After two minutes of chat room trivia and nasty comments from gamers, Simon grew bored and signed off. He thought of their young housekeeper Belle. Despite his father's insertion of a blocking program that was supposed serve as a "net nanny" he easily went through a secure browser to a soft porn web site. Then the sudden, roar of an aircraft passing directly overhead rattled the house and shattered his concentration on the virtual bare-breasted young women appearing on the monitor screen. The abrupt, distracting engine noise brought a momentary frown of annoyance and Simon left the computer to shut his second story bedroom window.

He glanced outside and his eyes held on the sturdy wooden dock that thrust from the island's rocky shore eighty-five feet into the deep inlet. His parents and Christa, his father's young executive assistant, were waiting by a stack of luggage. He knew he should sign off and say good-bye to his mother and father, but the lure of the young women on the large wall-mounted wide format, graphics quality monitor held him firmly. Simon took another look out the window before closing it.

@

What Simon failed to see was the late afternoon sun glinting off the water beyond the Greenlee's private dock and the tall stand of old growth cedars that marched majestically down to the shore ringing the family's island. Nor did he notice that in the shade of those ancient conifers a flourishing patch of wild late summer blackberries pregnant with sweet fruit sugar could still be found. With the window shut, he couldn't hear the caw of a raven startled by the floatplane's arrival, or smell the salty iodine odor of the clam flats exposed by an unusually low late summer tide.

At the seaward end of the long dock sat a two story boathouse that was used as the handyman's apartment. The sturdy wooden dock was the major artery supplying the family compound. Everything the Greenlees needed for their privileged comfortable life arrived by boat, barge or floatplane.

Food, mail, fuel for the generators and furnace, friends, business associates and the tons of building materials required to erect their imposing stone and timber mansion were unloaded on the dock of the self-contained island. Every one of the thousands of items needed to supply their wants and whims had to be hand-carted or carried up the wide flagstone path to the compound's kitchen, great room, dining hall, eight bedrooms, nine baths, Alex's office, and family home theater.

Jennifer Greenlee once feared that the enormous expense of building Alex's dream would bankrupt them, but her success-driven husband kept creating new cutting edge computer programs. Despite uncertain economic times his company grew more profitable each fiscal year.

Alex Greenlee needed the peace of mind that his secure and isolated island brought him. He slept well knowing that his twenty-five-hundred-and-fifty-seven acre forested estate was blocked from the turmoil of the urban mainland by dozens of islands and sixty-seven miles of salt water. The nearest residents, the owners of Yeager's rustic fish camp, lay a mile and a quarter beyond the island's north headland across the strait. The closest town, Friday Harbor, was half an hour to the east by fast boat. And the security patrol company Alex had engaged had the fastest boat in the area.

If any one of his five silent alarms sensed an intruder a satellite phone would automatically alert two armed San Juan Security guards based at Friday Harbor. In two minutes they would be on their way to investigate the alert. Alex had tested them several times and they always arrived, day or night, within half an hour. He slept better knowing they were dependable. Then a cloudy distant memory of a long ago deal gone sour brought a nagging worry, "With the merger there's going to be big time publicity I can't suppress. Perhaps it's time to have my own security guys on the island."

CHAPTER TWO

Alex had arranged his professional schedule, and the island's communication links, so he could run his company from the estate. He resented the increasing demands on his creative time brought about by the rapidly expanding and exceedingly profitable Greenlee Electronics empire. He especially disliked business trips and the marketing meetings they required. Today was different though. Alex was eagerly anticipating the flight to Holland and the coming merger with the giant electronics conglomerate Dutch Phillips.

Jennifer shared his enthusiasm for the journey. She often accompanied Alex on his travels, acting as his confidante and ego suppressor. She glanced at her husband. Admiring his erect posture and trim waistline that made him seem taller than his five foot ten inches, she thought, "Despite the stress of building his cyberdom, he's aging well. And not a bit of gray in his beard. After Holland..."

She silenced her brain chatter and eager expectations for their future. Later, when the merger was more than talk, she would realize her fantasizes about the enormous fortune that would gush unendingly from Alex's creations.

Celebration would come after the contracts were signed. Her job on this journey would be to keep her husband from becoming so overly aggressive he would blow the deal. And, it would be his biggest deal yet. Alex was wired that way, and his drive had thrust them further into the stratosphere of international mega-business than she had ever dreamed. With her dreams a reality she would have an art gallery in Manhattan, her loft studio in Soho, and the cultural stimulation this lonely island dream of Alex's so sorely lacked.

The pilot made a low pass over the dock and looked down to see Alex Greenlee waving at him. The Boss liked to have him buzz the estate. He guessed his client had never outgrown a youthful interest in flying. The pilot waved back and came about. He checked the wind direction and searched for boats or other aircraft. Except for a skiff heading for the dock it was clear to land. He pulled back the throttle and began a descent toward Greenlee's Island.

Alex stared at the 1960s era blue and white de Havilland Beaver floatplane and smiled faintly. When the weather was good, like today, he enjoyed flying the noisy, vibrating single engine aircraft. He turned to Christa and remarked, "What a classic. After Holland, I'm getting a pilot's license and my own floatplane."

"It's ancient," his young executive assistant said with distaste, "When I flew in here we bounced so much I thought I'd be airsick."

He ignored her complaint, "And not one computer chip aboard, except in the radio and navigation gear, but my God she still flies with authority."

He glanced at Christa and his smile faded. As usual when outdoors she wore a tennis cap with an oversize visor that protected her delicate pale sunscreen slathered skin. She was so unlike his beautiful long-limbed Jennifer who took the sun well and turned men's heads wherever they traveled. His wife seemed to grow more sensuous with each passing year. He wondered if Christa, despite her brilliance and organizational ability, had ever experienced any form of sensual pleasure.

Alex had worked closely with her for the last four years. He silently acknowledged his debt to Christa for the many contributions she'd made to the growth and expansion of Greenlee Electronics. On the several business trips they'd made together, it had never once occurred to Alex to sleep with her. Though Christa had an alluring figure hidden under her baggy jogging sweats that suggested potential sex, she was too much of a career-driven young executive to interest him, or most men. He sensed that Christa needed reassuring, "When the contracts are signed, I'll e-mail the good news. Hell no. I'll call you. You're a part of this, a big part."

"I would expect no less," she said without the slightest hint of emotion.

"Even Microsoft couldn't pull this off," Alex boasted with unusual pride, "In ten days Bill Gates will be blowing fuses."

"You've come a long way, Alex. No one else could have done it."

From Christa, that was high praise indeed. Alex switched his gaze from the stern woman and looked across the strait. His 20-foot outboard powered Alaska fishing skiff was cruising comfortably through the choppy water on a heading for the dock. The young man who had borrowed the boat to haul his gear from Simon's summer camp to the Greenlees' was skillfully guiding the sturdy skiff. Alex admired the boat's classic rough water hull. He'd had her built by a master craftsman in Yakutat, Alaska, and shipped down to Washington. The boat brought a smile, "Another little dream come true."

Alex waved at the approaching boatman and turned back to Christa, "Good. Tim's right on time. You'll like him. He was Simon's summer camp counselor."

"I can handle Simon."

"He obeys Tim, and Jennifer wants a dependable man around while we're gone."

Christa stared at the smiling young man in the skiff. He stood like a Viking, with one hand holding the outboard's tiller, taking the boat's pitching motions with graceful ease. She thought, "He's probably some brainless college jock on a football scholarship needing a place to stay until school starts. At least he looks fit enough to handle Simon."

Christa felt an unusual surge of resentment. Still looking at the boatman she thought, "I worked my way through Berkeley tutoring guys like him. And I studied my way out of that dusty Central Valley backwater farm town by winning a full four-year academic scholarship."

She wasn't pleased at the thought of sharing her authority over the compound with Simon's camp counselor, but Alex was boss, and his word was law if she wanted to reap the rewards that were certainly coming her way. With the Greenlee stock she already held, and those shares she had an option to purchase, she would become a very rich woman, "Stop thinking about it until it's all settled..."

Alex noticed her frown, "Lighten up. You're only here for ten days. Think of it as a paid vacation. You could use some sun and fresh air."

"I should be at the office."

"Run the company from here. You know the setup as well as I do."

Jennifer watched her husband talking with Christa and smiled faintly. She knew Alex had not the slightest twinge of sexual interest in

24

his young executive assistant, nor any other woman. Then she became conscious of Belle hovering behind her. Their young Haitian house keeper had an uncanny ability to arrive silently. With Belle, you felt her presence first. Jennifer turned to the slim twenty-five year old woman and saw her look of concern.

"Should I fetch Simon?" asked Belle in her soft French Creole accent.

"Please.

Belle nodded and turned to hurry down the dock to the compound's main house. Jennifer smiled as she watched their housekeeper of the past two years rush off. She truly liked the younger woman, despite Belle's reluctance to give up her bright Caribbean style and cook in a more traditional American way. Even Alex, whose meat and potato diet was conventional to the extreme, liked Belle's exotic cooking and her insistence on serving only fresh, organic vegetables she grew on the island.

To Jennifer, the usually cheerful woman was a tropic flower and a pleasing contrast to the somberness of the surrounding Pacific Northwest sea and forest. And Belle did love flowers. She had even talked Alex into having a greenhouse built so she could grow them and the fresh greens she proudly served all year long. Jennifer was glad to have found Belle but then she corrected herself, "Actually, it was Simon who found her."

On a furniture shopping trip to Seattle to buy couches for the new house, Jennifer had taken their son to the hair salon where Belle worked. Simon protested loudly that he didn't want his hair cut by a woman. Belle took charge and, by joking and teasing, she made his time in the hairdresser's chair fun. Later when their estate was finished, and Jennifer was interviewing housekeepers, Simon urged that they hire Belle. She had proved skillful and trustworthy ever since.

The snarl of the skiff's outboard motor blended with the deeper throb of the floatplane's powerful radial engine. Jennifer turned to watch Tim docking the open boat where it wouldn't interfere with the plane. She waved at the tanned young man and thought, "God, he's a handsome kid. No, not a kid. He's a few years older than he looks, probably because his skin takes the sun so well."

She felt a slight tightening of her stomach and realized that Tim had aroused her sexual interest. There was something about the young man that attracted her, and it wasn't his buff athlete's body. She sensed he had qualities of character that ran deeper than his good-natured exterior was showing. She felt a twinge of uncertainty about Tim being the right person to leave in charge of Simon. The camp director thought the world of Tim and Stanford Law School did verify he had a merit scholarship.

Shaking off her unusual mood she joined her husband. As usual, Tim was smiling. Alex and Jennifer said friendly hellos. Alex gestured to Christa, who was standing behind the Greenlees remaining aloof, and introduced her, "Tim, this is Christa Carter, my executive assistant. She'll be in charge here while we're gone."

"Hi, Christa," said Tim warmly.

She nodded curtly. Tim ignored her rudeness and glanced around the dock, "Where's Simon?"

The boy's parents looked uncomfortable until Jennifer broke the awkward moment, "Belle went to fetch him. He'll be here any minute."

Tim's concern wasn't satisfied, "But he's okay, isn't he?"

Jennifer picked up on that. "Of course he is. I wouldn't be traveling with Alex if he wasn't."

CHAPTER THREE

Belle ran through the opulent show place great room to the grand staircase that led to the second level. Even after two years, she was compelled to pause briefly by Mrs. Greenlee's collection of Northwest Native American artifacts. The priceless display was protected from touch and dust inside enormous glass cases. The expertly crafted remains of a dying culture — colorful ceremonial masks, shields, war clubs, spears, cedar storage boxes, feathered capes studded with glittering abalone shell, and a 1740 Russian iron trade axe — were so foreign to her that she always shuddered when passing them. Though Belle didn't believe in voodoo or the occult, there was something mystical about the blend of stylized animal representations and supernatural deities the north coast bands worshiped. She cast off her dark musing and raced on.

Belle dashed up the steps yelling, "Simon! Your parents are leaving! Outside! Right now. *Vite! Vite!*"

Belle found Simon on the couch staring at the monitor's electronically enhanced image of nude young women. She paused and shook her head. It wasn't the semi-naked girls he was focused on that troubled her. For a shy eleven-year-old it was natural. It was his collection of plastic power symbols that brought her frown. His room was much too war-like with its jumbled assortment of model battle tanks, toy broadswords, jet fighters, and an army of grotesque hand-painted in China figures of muscular professional wrestling celebrities. The only thing not made of synthetics was Simon's small English yew bow and its quiver of steel-tipped target arrows standing in a corner collecting dust.

The boy turned to stare at her. He exhibited no sense of shame or guilt for his interest in the young woman prancing across the screen. Abruptly, Belle reached beyond the boy and signed him off the web. He protested, "Belle, it's supposed to be my computer time."

She grabbed the boy by the arm, "Outside. To the dock. Hurry!"

@

On the dock, Tim was showing the Greenlees a packet of jumbo color prints he had taken with his Nikon on summer camp parents' day. Alex and Jennifer were impressed with Tim's photographic skill and complimented him on the pictures of Simon canoeing and competing in an archery contest. Tim handed the prints and a CD of the digital photos to Jennifer. His gift for them to take on their trip to Holland. She was touched by his thoughtfulness and said warmly, "We're so grateful that you got Simon to participate in outdoor activities, but he's gaining weight again."

Tim assured the boy's mother he'd have Simon slimmed down by the time they returned.

Alex turned to Christa and added, "He couldn't even paddle a canoe when camp started." With a glance at the fourteen foot canoe that sat upside down on a pair of low saw horses he said, "Since camp, Simon has taken the canoe out five times by himself, but she's starting to leak."

"I'll patch it while you're gone."

Tim gestured to Alex's wood-hulled 22 foot sloop *Jennifer* that was tied to the Greenlee dock, "And he'll be sailing her solo by the time you come back."

The young man sensed movement behind them and turned to see Belle driving Simon before her like a mother hen with a wayward chick. When the boy recognized Tim he rushed ahead to be with him.

As the floatplane nudged the dock, Simon stopped before his camp counselor and looked up at Tim without speaking. That was Simon's way. Tim put a hand on the boy's shoulder and softly said, "Give your folks a hug and kiss good-bye. We can talk later."

Belle caught up with Simon and gently shoved him toward his parents. With a frown the boy moved ahead to stand silently between them. Tim remained respectfully in the background and turned to steal a glance at Christa. She was frowning and he wondered if she ever smiled. He noted that her no-nonsense short brown hair was highlighted by the sun that also revealed tiny wrinkles around the outer edges of her greenish eyes.

That was a plus to Tim but the thick layer of sunscreen was certainly a turnoff. He liked older women and the slight signs of aging that gave them character. He watched the growing breeze flatten Christa's sweats against her body. She had a well shaped figure that the bulky cotton and polyester cloth couldn't hide.

Belle and Tim helped the pilot unload boxes of groceries and then stow the Greenlees' luggage into the plane. Simon moved to join them without helping. For a long moment he stood silently, staring at the pilot who finally noticed the boy. When their eyes met, Simon looked expectantly at the man in the worn World War II style leather flying jacket and asked in a hesitant high-pitched voice that was almost a squeak, "Is there mail today?"

The pilot appeared surprised and said, "Hey, thanks for reminding me."

He ducked into the cabin and came out with a US Postal Service plastic basket overflowing with mail and handed it to the boy. Simon eyed the large mix of junk advertising, manila envelopes, magazines and first class letters. Among them was a long cylindrical cardboard tube. He bent over the basket and looked closer. He spotted the small plastic mailer lined with bubble wrap he had been impatiently waiting for. He accepted the mail basket, murmured thanks to the pilot, and backed away. Simon checked the tube's mailing label and turned the round container so the sender's address would be hidden from view. When he was sure no one was watching he shoved the mailer out of sight. As the boy carried the basket up the dock toward the house his mother and father blocked his way.

Jennifer hunkered down before Simon and looked her son in the eyes. The boy knew that serious stuff was coming and waited patiently for his mother to speak.

"We'll be back in ten days. I'll miss you, Simon. Remember, Christa's in charge while we're gone."

The boy's face turned grim and she added, "So, mind her. Belle rules the kitchen. And no going in the water or woods unless Tim's with you."

When Simon didn't respond Alex gripped his shoulder, "Got it, Simon?"

"Got it, Dad."

Jennifer spoke quietly to Tim, "You can always reach us by e-mail. And do keep Simon outdoors and away from his computer, at least until dark."

"Hey, we'll have fun."

The pilot approached the group, "Any time you're ready."

As Jennifer started for the plane Alex put an arm around Simon. "I know I'm a bore about this, but..."

"Never give my password to anyone," Simon interrupted.

"And give those computer games a rest, okay?"

Satisfied that Simon knew the rules; his father gave the boy a final hug, entered the plane and took the seat beside the pilot. Alex always sat there. For the past two years he had absorbed both the feel and technique of piloting a floatplane. As soon as the de Havilland lifted off the water, Alex would take the right control wheel, fly the plane and ask the pilot endless questions. With the prospect of unending wealth Alex's dreams were expanding.

He envisioned his own floatplane tied to the dock. Then he would build an over-water hanger next to the boathouse and hire a mechanic to maintain the aircraft. He felt confident today and turned to the pilot, "Think I'm ready to try a take off?"

"The inlet's a little bumpy this afternoon. Just rest your hands on the wheel and throttle so you can feel what I'm doing. Next time we fly, if it's calm, it's your turn."

Tim moved quickly to free the floatplane's mooring lines and shove the pontoon away from the dock. A moment later the big radial engine barked into life. With the propeller blowing spray across the dock, the plane taxied away quickly gaining speed.

Tim and Belle stood together watching the aircraft hurtle across the choppy inlet. Then the floatplane's sturdy wings began to create lift and the pontoons left the water. There was a special fascination about all that heavy machinery overcoming gravity that neither of them could turn away from.

By the time the plane was on a heading for Seattle, Simon was already half way down the dock. Clutching the mail he hurried for the house and his computer. He had a plan, "First the poster, and then BAD WORLD. I can't wait, but I have to, until they go to bed. Oh. Wow. Gamer reviews have been all time cool."

Simon's fantastic ability to recall almost anything he ever read allowed him to murmur a quote from one of the reviewers, "You can grab a signpost, stab it through a guy's face, chuck him into a flaming bin... or hurl him head first at a human-size dartboard."

Simon hurried for the house and he called out to no one but himself, "Awesome!"

Christa, quickly growing bored and compulsively wanting to check in with her office at Greenlee Electronics, followed the boy. At the high pitched sound of Simon's voice she wondered what was so 'awesome' in the container of mail he was protectively clutching.

Tim and Belle remained on the dock watching the plane disappear into the wispy stratus clouds of the late afternoon sky. When the sound of its throbbing engine at last faded away, they remained by the water absorbing the silence and the island's brooding isolation.

@

There was one other person on the island watching the plane depart. An old man, born in Finland seventy-eight years ago, stood on a slight rise behind the main house. As usual Karl Mannheim was frowning.

He had never flown in a plane and didn't intend to fly in one now. The Greenlee's combination grounds keeper, handyman, and gardener held a long two-handled wooden scythe. He ran a scarred finger bent almost double with arthritis along the curved steel blade and found it needed sharpening. He liked his lonely existence and the quiet of the island.

Now two strangers had arrived and they would soon be disturbing his peace with damn fool questions. And the young man was given Karl's room over the boathouse. Karl was now sleeping in a guest cabin where he couldn't hear the soothing lap of water against the dock pilings.

Karl pulled a sharpening stone from the bib pocket of his overalls, touched up the scythe's blade, and returned to cutting grass. He liked his job. For every two weeks work on the island he was given a week off. Mr. Greenlee paid well and allowed him the time to restore the old sloop he kept at Friday Harbor. When she was fully seaworthy Karl was planning to sail the boat back to Finland. His frown eased, "I never imagined I'd work for a man who hates the sound of chainsaws and grass mowers as much as I do."

CHAPTER FOUR

Alex Greenlee sat beside the pilot holding the right side control wheel. He was in command of the aircraft for now and enjoying the sensation of directing the old Beaver on a south easterly heading for Seattle. Turning the wheel, and toeing the rudder, he sent the plane in a shallow bank that allowed him a final look at his island. The massive house was now a small patch of brown timber and gray stone surrounded by green forest and white-capped salt water. The long dock had become a pencil thin line projecting into the inlet.

He shifted his eyes to the island's center where the small shimmering rock-rimmed lake broke the dense stand of cedars. Near the center of the kidney shaped island, the land thrust upward nearly nine-hundred-feet collecting rain that drained into the lake. That was high ground for the San Juans. The hill's elevation was noted on local nautical and aviation charts, but so far had remained nameless. Alex thought about asking the U.S. Coast and Geodetic Survey Director to designate his hill Mount Greenlee, but on second thought, he felt that was a bit much and might compromise his security.

Alex had a plan for the lake. When there was time, he would build with his own hands a small log cabin along the shore. There would be no electricity, no phones, and no modern conveniences. He wanted no reminders of the complex urban world to intrude on the privacy he desired. Light would come from kerosene lamps, heat from a fireplace. In the primitive cabin beside the pristine lake, Alex envisioned that he would unplug from the stress of his competitive corporate world and not even a solar powered laptop would be allowed.

The pilot gave Alex a course change to avoid a commercial aircraft corridor. He checked the compass and turned the floatplane on a new heading for Seattle. They would land on Lake Union, then take a waiting limo to SeaTac International Airport, and jet off in pampered first class comfort for Holland. When he brought the plane to its cruising altitude of three-thousand five-hundred feet, Alex could see most of the hundreds of San Juan Islands. Friday Harbor, the main town of San Juan Island itself, showed clearly to the west and was constantly expanding into the forested interior. Sweeping vistas of dark green firs, clear blue lakes that mirrored the trees and hills, steep cliffs that plunged to the rocky shoreline, and even the orchards and farm fields ready for fall harvest, gave Alex a sense of deep satisfaction.

His isolation from the relentless press of development and the hundreds of thousands of tourists who besieged the San Juans every summer clouded the reality of what was occurring around his island. Alex didn't read the local papers. He was only vaguely aware that real estate agents were touting the area as the high status "Martha's Vineyard" of the Pacific Northwest.

Old time locals who resented the ever increasing wealthy retired and new rich population, but still sold off overpriced lots complained bitterly about greedy developers. So far Alex was safe from sub-dividers and the constant stream of weekend boaters who sailed past his island for the Friday Harbor Marina and the town's quaint commercial charms. He had little to do with the community. With a frown of concern he thought that in the coming year it might be wise to make friends and political connections to ensure that his island's sanctity would not be violated by a well-meaning environmental group wanting to turn it into a nature reserve.

Farther to the northwest the outline of vast Vancouver Island, British Columbia, Canada, thrust skyward. Even at this great distance Alex could make out the ravaged clear cut slopes of the island's mountainous interior. Timber companies had left a green belt around the shore to screen the massive destruction caused by unregulated logging and the crudely bulldozed dirt roads that caused such widespread land damaging erosion. From the air the rape of the island's timber forests was all too apparent. His island had never been logged, except for the few ancient cedars, almost ready to topple, that were felled for house timbers. Alex was forever thankful that the previous owners had resisted selling logging rights to the always ready to buy and clear-cut lumber companies.

His island's old growth cedar forests were easily worth a fortune. A single mature tree, if its value was fairly judged, would bring fifteen to twenty thousand dollars where it stood. Alex considered the trees a living continually growing savings provision that would forever prohibit the felling of Greenlee Island trees for profit. More than anything else on the island, the old growth cedars were the symbol of his hard fought power and independence.

He hoped Simon would grow up to respect the forest and every living thing on the island. Last year he hired a biologist from the University of Washington to survey the island's plant and animal life. Alex walked the island with Simon and the scientist. They were amazed by the rich natural diversity they found. Raccoons, beavers, otters, mice and rats, rabbits and chipmunks, deer and the occasional bear all flourished. In the trees nested horned owls, golden and bald eagles, osprey and hawks. Migrating mallards, hooded mergansers and harlequin ducks landed to rest in the sheltered inlet and on the freshwater lake.

Along the shore the biologist had pointed out a colony of harbor seals, a pair of sea otters, and beds of little-neck geoduck and butter clams. In deeper water were octopus, dungeness crabs, oysters, and dozens more inter-tidal species. Off the island swam gray whales on their way north to the Bering Sea or south to give birth in the warm secure lagoons of Mexico's Baja California. From the island's shore they had spotted giant orca feeding on passing salmon. He thought, "The salmon might all pass out of existence if we don't stop over-fishing and polluting the sea."

Alex remembered that Simon did show interest when the biologist explained the relationship between predator and prey, and how it related to the overall balance of nature. Best of all was the discovery that a small run of wild Chinook salmon spawned in the quiet waters that flowed from the island's lake.

The steady throb of the engine calmed Alex. He dreamed on, imagining himself catching a salmon from the front porch of his cabin, but only one to broil over an alder wood fire for a supper he would prepare for Jennifer. The cabin would be their secret retreat where they could talk, dream, swim nude, make love, and dine on the fish he caught for her.

He wondered if his son would ever look at the island's tall straight-trunked cedars as ancient giants that stood bravely bending as storm after storm beat against their swaying crowns. When they had explored the island with the biologist the only animals that seemed to impress Simon were the giant orca and playful sea otters.

Alex questioned whether he might have made a mistake keeping Simon out of school and trusting his education to one tutor after another, who would arrive at the island to teach the boy the basics of math, English, and the physical sciences. Once Simon had mastered the computer and learned to thread his way through the Internet, he proved a brilliant student and began teaching himself. But what was he learning about life?

His thoughts shifted to a memory of climbing to the island's crest. Alex had been caught in a driving northwesterly gale and took shelter under the trees. Pressing against a gnarled, moss-covered trunk that had withstood battering storms for six hundred years, he found protection from pelting hale as big as golf balls that smashed down with sufficient force to flatten whole beds of fiddle ferns. He remembered looking upward and being awed by the sight of the crowns of the high trees veiled by storm clouds. He wondered if his son would ever be moved by nature. If not, then what would awe him?

He knew that Simon was truly brilliant. Though the boy was overweight and only eleven years old, he had learned almost all his father could teach him about cyberspace. But why didn't his son ever go outdoors and comb the beach, or wander the island unless forced to, or break a window, or cry, or even laugh at Saturday morning TV cartoons, or demand the latest kid fad toy. Never. For Simon laughter came from watching grotesque wrestlers beat each other up. Excitement came from the challenge of playing computer games. Jennifer accepted the boy as he was, but Alex wanted him to be a real son and not some Internet addicted robot like the fawning young men he employed.

The pilot nudged Alex and gestured to something a few degrees off the nose of the Beaver. "Ah, Mister Greenlee. Check out that Piper Apache on our heading. You might want to veer a bit to starboard...."

He saw the approaching plane's blinking strobe lights and realized they were on a collision course. Overcoming his surprise, Alex banked the old Beaver smoothly to the right.

Although Alex Greenlee was his best customer the pilot cautioned, "It's all too easy to daydream up here. And we're approaching Seattle, so I'll take over now. When you return we'll get serious about teaching you to fly."

Alex didn't want to release the control wheel. He was always in control, but reason overcame his ego. He reluctantly turned command over to the pilot and allowed his mind to return to Simon.

He felt Jennifer's hand rest gently on his shoulder. Her gentle fingertips were sending signals that he recognized. She could sense when he was growing tense and her touch helped to soothe him. She knew that look. He was worrying about Simon. He wanted him to be like other boys. But Alex wasn't at all like other men. Nor was their son like other children.

Simon, she thought, was too damn smart for his own good. Jennifer promised herself that upon their return she would take charge of the boy, wean him away from cyberspace, and send him off to boarding school where he would be forced to get along with kids his own age. She thought the rough and tumble of some outdoor, back-to-nature school with high academic standards might shock him into the real world.

But what was the real world anymore? With never ending wars and the current economic turmoil, life in the United States was going to hell. If Alex's creation actually were to be universally adopted it would change the world and neither their son's life nor theirs would ever be normal. They'd be climbing aboard a golden rocket that would take them to the apogee of wealth and power.

CHAPTER FIVE

Christa walked into the house and paused to glance about the vast living room that was hardly ever used. The back bricks of the massive stone fireplace, with its rare myrtle wood mantel, were free of soot and as clean as when the masons had laid them three years ago. The fireplace in the family room off the kitchen was the one that was blackened and had ash under the log grate. She wondered why Alex and Jennifer needed such a showplace. "For all the entertaining they do a mobile home would serve just fine."

Christa suddenly realized she was hungry and turned to the huge kitchen-breakfast area, where the family usually ate with Belle. For the money they had spent on the latest German Gaggenau hob and ovens, double size SubZero refrigerator, industrial mixers, juicers, vegetable grinders, trash compactor, and espresso bar, all controlled by one of Alex's computer driven master command centers, an average income family could have built a small house. The Greenlees did eat well, thanks to Belle's marvelous Haitian cooking and the organic vegetables she grew in the greenhouse.

Christa didn't want a gourmet meal, "Something simple, like ham and Swiss cheese on rye bread and a beer without Belle hovering around trying to spice it up with her voodoo Haitian hot sauces."

She needed both hands to open the refrigerator's main door and cautioned herself, "Don't binge now or you'll blow up like a balloon."

She found the cheese, a packet of thin sliced Danish ham, mayonnaise, French mustard and whole wheat bread Belle had baked yesterday. She had ground the flour from organic wheat berries in an electric mill. With appreciation, Christa smelled the yeasty fresh bread slightly sweetened with honey, then laid her sandwich makings on a cutting board and ripped off the plastic wrappings. She could do without supermarket rye. She stuffed a rolled slice of ham into her mouth and smiled for the first time that day. She might be bored here, but she would never starve at the Greenlees.

@

Tim sat on the rough fir planks of the dock and let his legs dangle over the water. He motioned for Belle to join him. After a long moment staring across the inlet he broke the island's moody silence, "With camp over, and a couple of weeks until school starts, this is a lucky break for me."

"Back to California?"

"Stanford. Final year of law school. Mister Greenlee said they were off to Holland, some sort of merger with Dutch Phillips, is that right?"

Belle laughed softly and said, "Always computer business. Never have I seen Mister Greenlee so, ah *excite*."

Tim turned to gaze at the house and added, "Quite a world they've created for themselves here."

44

"Tres magnifique, yes?"

The house was magnificent. From the dock, at water level, it appeared lower than its two stories. The artfully mortised dark granite stone walls of the first floor and weather grayed wood planked second story blended harmoniously with the conifer forest that thrust upward beyond the wide backyard. The basic design, that Alex had of course laid out on his computer, suggested 18th Century New England. Tim noticed a few weeds sprouting on the wide front lawn that flowed downward to the dock and shore. He turned to Belle and asked, "There's a lot to take care of here. Don't the Greenlee's have a gardener?"

Belle stood and looked beyond the main house. A bright dazzle of reflected light bounced off the scythe's blade. She indicated a tall older man cutting grass on the hill behind the house, "There he is, swinging that steel blade back and forth. Karl can do that for hours."

Tim studied the old man's smooth movements admiring his skill. Then the man stopped. Even at this distance Tim sensed the gardener was looking at him. Karl abruptly returned to his work. Tim remarked, "He looks like the grim reaper up there."

"That's what Simon calls Karl. Be nice to him. He gave up his room above the boathouse so you could have private quarters."

"Does he live here full-time?"

"Two weeks on, then a week off. He'll sail off in two days and return a week later. Imagine, a gardener coming to work by boat."

He studied the "grim reaper" carefully. Belle noticed his concentration and asked Tim why he was so curious about the gardener. Tim returned from a far off mind trip and carefully answered, "He may be the last one around here that still knows how to use a scythe. I wonder if he'd teach me."

"Good luck. He may be a bit miffed at having to move his stuff so you can have the boathouse.".

With a laugh Tim got to his feet and dropped lightly into Alex's Alaska rough water skiff. "Better get my gear inside. Is the power on there?"

"Always on. We have back up for the back up generators."

She pointed to the mansion's already weathered gray slate roof where several dish antennas stood outlined against the pale blue sky. "He even has a satellite up link for the phones and television. We have everything."

"Except cars."

Tim turned to reach for his backpack and the boxes in green plastic waterproofed garbage bags. Belle stood and asked, "Need some help unloading?"

"What I need is lunch."

"As soon as you're settled, head for the kitchen."

"Is the boathouse open?"

Belle reached for a key fixed to a lanyard that hung around her neck and handed it to Tim. "I almost forgot. Mr. Greenlee wants the boathouse locked at night. One of his favorite toys is floating inside. Oh, he wants the skiff kept inside, too. And, there's an electric heater upstairs in case it turns chilly."

"*Merci, ma Cherie*, and that's all the French I know."

Belle turned, loaded the boxes of groceries onto a hand cart and started for the house. Tim watched her walk off and then reached into the boat for his things. He tossed his sturdy forest green canvas backpack onto the dock, then carefully lifted the plastic covered boxes and gently set them down on the wooden planking.

@

Nibbling her sandwich, Christa walked slowly along the long hall that led to the grand staircase. She paused to study Jennifer's collection of north coast Indian artifacts. Running her fingers along the tall glass cases she murmured, "There are things here people shouldn't have, no matter how rich they are. All that priceless stuff belongs in a museum."

She took another step, glanced at the last doorway down the hall and froze. "What in hell is that?"

She moved quickly now, almost at a run, and stopped to stare at a new gray metal door that used to be planked cedar. She tapped her fingernails on its smooth, dull gray surface, "Steel."

Inside, she knew, was Alex Greenlee's private office and design studio. In the solitude of his work space Alex's creative ideas flowed. The vault-strong metal door was new, as were two maximum security locking devices. Christa had seen similar locks at Greenlee Electronics. She recognized the signature recognition pad and the retina scanner. Inside would be another silent alarm connected by a dedicated microwave transmitter to the local security company.

Alex must be feeling paranoid, or there's been an actual attempt to break in.," she thought. "So, how in hell am I going to get inside and work on our project?"

CHAPTER SIX

Christa sensed someone behind her and turned to see Belle. "New security, Belle? When did Mister Greenlee have these installed?"

"Two weeks ago. When Tim brought Simon home from camp. He had all that stuff flown in. Then Mister Greenlee and Tim put the door in together and he loaned Tim the skiff."

"Did he leave instructions about how to override the locks?"

"Nobody unlocks Mister Greenlee's work room except Mr. Greenlee."

Christa turned to peer at the retina scanner. The locking device was almost one-hundred percent foolproof. If the optical sensor didn't recognize the individual's eyes the door would remain locked. Additional security was achieved with the signature recognition pad. Signatures could be forged, but not the way each person moved the signing stylus. To have one's signature identified by the recognition pad, the authorized individual wrote his name ten times. The computer program held a record of distinct hand movements, and pressure exerted on certain letters of the designated individual's hand writing the signature.

Christa again faced Belle and said, "That's not like Alex. Why do you suppose...?"

"He's been acting strange lately, like he doesn't trust anyone. I'm sure it's not personal."

Christa wondered if Belle was slighting her, or just being innocently frank. She let it pass and walked around the bronze-skinned woman for the grand staircase. Going up the wide carpeted steps she wondered if the exotic Haitian was a threat to her authority. She suspected that Alex found Belle sexually attractive, but rejected the idea.

Passing by the door to Simon's room, she glanced inside. She saw the boy standing on his desk Scotch taping a wrestler's poster to the blonde wood paneling.

She loathed the aggressive, loud-mouthed muscle-bound performers and considered interfering. "Not my job. Let Tim handle him."

She walked the long sterile white hallway that Jennifer had yet to decorate with art from local landscape painters. In the large guest apartment overlooking the inlet that would be her home for the next ten days she took a deep breath of resignation, "Oh, well. Better than a computer convention in Las Vegas."

Alex had carefully planned the office guest-suite where Christa was staying for dual use. She knew her boss always had a 'Plan B'. If Greenlee Electronics went belly up the estate could be quickly converted to a high end fishing lodge. The main house had seven identical bedroom suites with ocean and forest views to pamper paying guests escaping the stress of mainland living. Even Simon had his own apartment with its bath and sauna. Alex was inspired by Walt Disney who had built his studio to be converted into a hospital should his big budget animated films fail. She remembered Alex saying, "Old Walt was as sharp as they come, he'd do well with either laughter or sickness."

On a large solid wood work station sat HP's latest terabyte computer, so new she hadn't used one before. She frowned, "How long is it going to take me to learn this one?" Christa did appreciate the wide screen Sony HD monitor, printer/scanner, fax, two-line video-conference and speaker phone, and digital tape deck to discreetly record conversations.

She was also connected to the Seattle home office by the company's private intranet system and video conferencing link. Her own laptop sat on a small table by the bed along with several technical books she intended to read. The room even had a wet bar, refrigerator, mini-espresso machine and coffee bean grinder. Christa opened the refrigerator. It was well stocked with fruit juices, mineral waters, beer, small bottles of white wine, salty snacks and three varieties of organic free-trade coffee beans. Alex had anticipated her preferences. That was reassuring.

Christa was restless. In this new environment she couldn't face sitting in front of the computer and writing another memo about corporate security and the threat of hackers entering their system's mainframe. She turned to an open window and gazed across the water at the green forested islands beyond. Movement on the dock drew her eyes to the boathouse where Tim was locking the door. As he walked off she wondered why he would lock the boathouse in daylight or at any time on the Greenlee's secluded island.

A reflection of her face on the window glass revealed the thick coating of sunscreen she had applied before going outside. Christa shook her head, "Am I overdoing this? A little sun can't hurt, and I look awful." She hurried to the bathroom and scrubbed her face. "No wonder that Tim person gave me a funny look."

@

Belle carried fresh baked oatmeal pecan cookies and a glass of milk up to her lavish room. Sometimes she and Simon met in the housekeeper's quarters at the far end of the upstairs hall. As a reminder of home she had hung several large brightly colored prints of Haitian primitive art on the walls. Simon liked the exaggerated rural scenes which allowed Belle a springboard into telling him stories about her previous island life and the trauma of the great earthquake.

On her desk were an old German Olympia push-key manual portable typewriter that Simon made fun of, framed photos of her family, and a collection of books, mostly in French. She had a few classic novels printed in English which she urged Simon to enjoy, but LED screens and computer game magazines were all he was interested in reading.

They had developed an informal late afternoon ritual of getting together to talk about life and the outside world. Belle felt it was important to broaden the boy's horizons so he would know something of the world beyond Greenlee's island. Simon liked to ask her questions about what it was like living in Haiti and how she and her family survived the earthquake. They would sit on her bed close together. He snuggled against her as he listened carefully. "As I explained before, we lived some ten kilometers from Port au Prince on a hill overlooking the Caribbean. Our house was timber so the wood frame bent and shook instead of breaking as concrete did."

"Tell me about the cockroaches."

He often asked for this and she obliged him. "About a minute before the quake hit hundreds of cockroaches began scurrying out of the woodwork. They ran in circles utterly confused, as did the mice. Then our cat, instead of attacking the mice, began mewing and the dog started howling..."

"Because they sensed the earthquake was coming! If we could train cockroaches to alert us far enough in advance, think of it! We could train them to live in abandoned oil wells, or gold mines. They like the dark and we'd keep them alive with food and water. We'd have sensors to pick up their earthquake coming signals. Wow! What a business that would be. And we'd save lives and property."

"Perhaps you'll do that, Simon."

"Then what happened Belle?"

She knew he liked this part best and gave it special emphasis, "Everything that wasn't fastened or tied down went sailing through the air to smash on the floor... glasses, pots, a jar of honey, family pictures, even my grandfather's false teeth..."

Simon giggled. Belle frowned, "It wasn't funny at the time. There were so many dead and we were all worried sick about my father..."

"...Because he was in prison for his political activities."

"In his newspaper columns he opposed the government and exposed their corruption."

"And the secret police were after you as well..."

"As you know, that's why I'm here. Do you remember what I told you?"

"They wanted you as a hostage to force your father to confess that he was a communist terrorist, and you and your father escaped during the earthquake."

"Though the earthquake killed thousands and destroyed much of

Port au Prince…

"Including the prison…"

"…the enormous disruption helped us reach safety."

"Where is your father now?"

"The last I heard he's in Cuba. He has many friends and they helped me escape as well… and so here I am. And you must never never mention what I've told you to anyone."

Belle was pleased to share her experiences from another world, another life, so different a life from his. Simon, in turn, was teaching Belle the basics of word processing. When Belle had asked for his help she explained, "I won't always be a housekeeper. I'll need your skills."

"And I won't always be a kid. When I'm older we could run away together. We'll have plenty of money because I'll be half partner in Greenlee."

She feigned shock but was secretly delighted by his innocent frankness. "How you talk for an eleven-year-old."

He grinned, "And going through puberty soon."

She seemed surprised. He added, "They inject those growth hormones in beef and dairy cattle. That's why girls get sexy really early."

"How do you know all this, Simon?"

"With the Internet, kids know everything."

Bell took a breath and asked Simon what she had been asking him everyday for almost a year, "Any message for me?"

He knew she was desperate to hear from her father and as always he answered, "Unless you had a prearranged code that wouldn't alert the cyber watchers, he'd stay off the Internet. My dad says he knows his e-mail's monitored by the Feds."

Today Simon had something else on his mind besides Belle's body.

As they munched cookies he said off-handedly, "I heard Mom and Dad talking about sending me away to boarding school..."

She decided not to comment and waited for him to reveal what was really going on. Without displaying any emotion the boy remarked, "I don't want to go away. I want to stay here with you."

"I won't always be working here, and you're missing the world, Simon."

"I can learn everything I need to know at the computer."

"That machine can't teach you about real life, or what a sunset feels like in the Caribbean, or how to look people in the eye and tell if they're lying or not."

Not liking her logic, Simon folded his arms over his chest and pouted.

"Simon, you're missing so much on this island. It's like you're locked inside a big bubble. You have no friends to play with. You've got to know things, real things. And the world is always changing. If you don't know, don't have life experiences, they can get you."

"Who's they?"

"People who will take advantage of you because you don't know about people."

He bought her logic, "Will I learn about that in boarding school?"

"And a lot more."

"Okay, I'll go away to school when I have to."

She put down her cookie and hugged the boy. He liked being drawn against her, "I love you, Belle."

CHAPTER SEVEN

Tim also paused by Jennifer's glass cased artifact collection. He knew a bit about the Bella Coola, Makah, and Kwakiutl cultures. He admired the skill of the artisans who had carved the masks and decorated them with such bold, primary colors. The crude iron hand axe, he knew, was 17th Century Russian, traded to north coast Indians for sea otter pelts. The early Russian explorers and First Americans were tough people, "If they'd gotten along, I'd probably be speaking Russian today."

Tim walked on and up the staircase looking for Simon. It was just too nice out on the water and somehow he was going to get the kid to catch a salmon. He wondered how the boy would react with a big Chinook on his line.

On the way upstairs, he glanced at the massive cedar timbers holding up the second story. The huge twelve by eighteen inch beams were sixty feet long and all straight grain wood clear of knots. He had heard that when Alex Greenlee bought the island he selected several old, already dying cedars to be felled for the house. Then loggers with chainsaws carefully dropped the massive trees so they wouldn't crush the younger ones. Later, a portable sawmill was shipped to the island and the long timbers were custom cut for the building. As Tim admired the beams he thought, "Except for the house, and felling those old cedars, the island's probably the way it was a thousand years ago."

Tim found the boy on the couch working the keyboard composing an e-mail. He remained in the doorway to let his eyes wander the room. He scanned Simon's huge library of video games. Simon was a Sony Play Station guy. On Simon's desk three game boxes caught Tim's attention: THE HOUSE OF THE DEAD, OVERKILL and BAD WORLD. Tim made a rough estimate of the cost of Simon's library of video games, "Maybe two-thousand dollars worth. Alex's credit card must have taken a major hit." Then Simon noticed Tim's shadow, "I'm sending a thank you e-mail to Crusher."

"The guy on the poster?"

Simon nodded and motioned Tim to sit on the couch. Tim scanned Simon's brief note on the huge monitor.

Dear Crusher,
The poster arrived and thanks. I watched your
last match on TV. You were great. I'm designing
a computer game and you're the action hero.
Your friend, Simon

He faced Tim, wanting a critique. It came at him hard and relentless. "My God, Simon. Getting involved with all that phony TV wrestling crap. You're smarter than that. Look at your setup here. You're wasting a really cool opportunity to put all this to work. Really explore the web. Take on-line courses, learn something besides gaming. Make some friends of real kids, like the guys you met at camp."

Simon went on the defensive, "I'm in a chat room every day, and on Facebook. You know, social network stuff."

"Out of my range, Simon."

"You're not on Facebook!"

"I don't have time for that stuff."

"You might miss an important connection with someone."

Tim grew serious, "I value my privacy much more than connecting with a stranger."

Simon nodded understanding, "My dad's the same way. He won't let anyone into his life, or even visit here, that he doesn't know personally."

Tim thought on that, "You know, your dad and I have a lot in common."

"Yeah, you're both old fashioned guys who like their privacy. Of course, Dad has a reason to stay off the radar. But that's going to change. It won't be long before everyone will be under a universal computer umbrella hooked up to a giant worldwide gazillion byte mainframe."

"And there goes privacy, and every government will know what everyone is doing in real time, but that's a long way off, Simon.

"Not so, Tim. It'll be sooner than you think."

Tim challenged, "And how about languages? Can a kid in Guatemala connect with the girl in Canada so they both can understand each other?"

For once the boy showed a faint smile of pleasure. "It's going to work for everyone. Dad's new operating system is going to create that global umbrella. Everyone will want it and any dummy can learn it."

"Even this dummy?"

Tim's joke produced a mild giggle which the boy quickly suppressed.

"But really soon you won't even need to type stuff in. Dad's system's going to blow Microsoft and Apple right out of the water."

"Really?"

"It's a big Greenlee Corporation secret."

Tim put a hand on Simon's shoulder and said, "Well then, let's keep it that way. Maybe I should know something about social networking. Is there a Facebook type of site for lawyers?"

They felt Belle's presence behind them. How long had she been standing there listening to them? Neither man nor boy could guess, but her annoyance was more than clear.

"Didn't you two hear me call? Supper's ready. Tim, you get Simon away from that thing and downstairs. *Vite. Vite.* And I don't mean maybe."

Two minutes, Belle," said Tim with an accommodating smile.

In the kitchen Belle slammed platters onto a wheeled serving cart. She glanced at Christa, who had not made a move to help, and said, "Lots of fresh vegetables tonight and broiled free-range chicken, Haitian style."

When Christa only nodded Belle poured a glass of milk for Simon and added, "Always that boy's frying his brain and burning his eye balls. You should see that game stuff he plays. People killing people, car crashes, monsters screaming, and guns, always guns going off. God only knows what it is doing to his little soul. And there's no one for him to play with or do boy things with. Christa, you'd better get Tim to do his thing."

"Yes, of course. I'll speak with him after supper."

Belle put the glass of milk on the cart and turned to slide four whole wheat rolls into the oven. Her annoyance was growing by the second, and watching the Yankee watch her only increased Belle's ire. In her sweet, condescending Creole accent, Belle told the other woman, "If you've got a moment, *Cherie*, roll the cart outside and put supper on the table while I fix Karl's tray. He'll come by for it later."

"Does he always eat alone?"

"Since the day he arrived. He's a strange old guy."

"Is he dangerous?"

"All I know is he's seventy-some years old, from Finland, and likes to sail his little, ah, *bateau a voile*."

That bit of intelligence satisfied Christa and she filed it away in a category of things not to fear. She turned from Belle, opened the refrigerator and took out a half liter bottle of Pellegrino mineral water. She checked the expiration date to assure the water was potable and asked, "Where do you keep the bottle opener, Belle?"

Belle shoved the cart to the door that led to the sea facing patio and said, "Being Mister Greenlee's executive assistant and all, Miss Christa, I expect you're smart enough to see that bottle you're holding has a twist off cap."

Despite the spectacular view across the inlet, and a formation of honking Canadian geese flying above the patio on their way south, Tim noticed the tension between the two women. He tried to lift the mood and turned to Simon, "Hey, the Chinook are running. What do you say we take the skiff out tomorrow and catch a couple of salmon?"

Belle brightened. "*Tres Bien*. I'll cook them like at home, with peppers and mangos."

"I hate fish," said Simon, deflating the chance for uplifting the supper conversation.

Tim said with unusually strong feeling, "Well, I like salmon. And tomorrow I'm taking the skiff out and catching our supper. And Simon,

61

you are coming with me."

Hearing the strength of Tim's order, Simon knew he'd go fishing with him tomorrow and agreed. The boy gulped down the last of his milk and slid his chair back from the table. He moved to leave, but Christa stood and blocked his way. "And just where do you think you're going?"

"To my room. What's it to you, Christa?"

She placed her hands on the boy's shoulders and shoved him back into his chair. "Give cyberspace a rest, Simon."

With a stern glance at Tim she added, "And, since it's still light, Tim will take you on a short hike."

When Simon scowled Christa said, "It's a hike or clear the table and load the dishwasher."

Tim said, "Go get your jacket. It's getting cold."

Obeying Tim, the boy left the table. When Simon was out of earshot Christa laid down the law to Tim, "You are not a guest here. You've got a job to do. Indulge that kid and he'll take advantage of you every time."

"Got it, Christa. Want to go on a hike?"

"I'd rather do the dishes."

He turned to Belle, "Since Christa's cleaning up, how about coming with us?"

The Haitian woman laughed softly. Turning to Christa she said, "Ah, *Cherie*, how kind you are to give the help some time off."

CHAPTER EIGHT

The three hikers hurried down the wide flagstone steps that led to the island's rocky, driftwood strewn shore. Simon looked back at the sea-facing patio. Christa was sitting in a chair and not a dish had been removed from the table. The boy paused. He considered yelling at her to get to work, but Tim and Belle were moving ahead. In his slow lumbering way he ran to catch up. Simon noticed he became quickly out of breath. "They're right. I have to lose some weight. I'll lose five pounds and surprise mom and dad when they get back."

Half a mile to the north, where a rocky headland jutted into the strait blocking their way along the shore, Tim paused and pointed to the water. After a moment of staring at the thick fronds of bullhorn kelp that grew off the beach Simon sighted a pair of sea otters swimming through the thick mat of growth. Tim whispered, "They're playful little guys, but if they've got pups, don't go swimming near them, because they'll bite."

Simon nodded without expressing any emotion and Tim turned away from the shore to lead them inland. Away from the beach, where tall old growth cedars grew thick and little of the day's final sunlight filtered through their tall crowns, the boy felt uneasy. Simon moved closer to Tim and Belle and pushed between them. He noticed that Tim's eyes swept the forest as if searching for unseen dangers. Simon had never been this far inland so late in the day and the oppressive, damp gloom was not to his liking.

Feeling more and more insecure, Simon zipped his international rescue orange windbreaker to the neck. The warm waterproof coat was a gift from his father, who hoped that the expensive action sports jacket might inspire his son to become more active outdoors. Simon wanted the safety of his room and the comfort of the glowing video screen. Then he saw Tim pause and kneel by a patch of damp soil yet to be overgrown by brambles. Simon crouched beside Tim and looked at what he had found.

Tim's fingers rested by cloven hoof tracks and he looked up at Simon and Belle. "A buck and a doe. They probably swam here from the mainland 'cause the browsing's good, or maybe to escape hunters."

"Hunters?" asked Simon with a hint of interest.

"Yeah, deer season just started. Come on. Let's follow their tracks."

The hoof prints led deeper into the interior of the island where rocky outcroppings thrust upward preventing the growth of trees. Here lichen, blackberry and salmon berry vines, and fiddle ferns grew in rare patches of open ground where sunlight warmed them. At the edge of a glade Tim reached out and stopped Simon and Belle. He put a finger to his lips cautioning silence and pointed to the far side of the clearing.

Twenty yards away an antlered black-tailed buck and a doe browsed on ferns, seemingly unconcerned by the arrival of the three humans. Simon's eyes went wide and he wondered if the deer could sense they were not hunters. After a moment the buck raised his head to look directly at them.

His ears twitched and he nuzzled the doe as if to tell her something. Without the slightest hurry or display of panic, the two deer slowly walked off and vanished into the thick brush. The boy turned to Tim and whispered, "Will they have babies?"

"In the spring."

"Are they safe from hunters here?" asked Belle.

Before Tim could answer the boy said forcefully, "They're on our island, so they're our deer, and there's no hunting allowed here."

"They could come by boat and never be seen. How could you stop them?" asked Tim.

"Make it open season on hunters," the boy said with unusual intensity.

Tim looked into Simon's narrowed, angry eyes, and saw something of himself, "Hunters have guns."

The boy responded quickly, "I'll make 'No Hunting' signs on my computer. I'll print up a bunch and we can tack them up all around the island."

Tim nodded approvingly and turned to lead them back. Simon was smiling now.

@

In the kitchen Tim pulled open the heavy refrigerator door and spotted a row of German Beck's beers and grabbed a pair of bottles. As Belle watched, he pulled a Swiss Army knife from his jeans, uncapped the bottles and handed her one. He noticed that the outside patio table had been cleared, but the dishes were piled in the sink waiting to be rinsed and loaded into the washer. Tim looked from the dishes to Belle, who shrugged and took a sip of beer. At the kitchen table, Simon was spooning down ice cream and reading the latest edition of Computer Gaming that had arrived with the mail.

When Christa entered she glanced at the three and then turned to the kitchen sink. "The dishes, Belle."

"*Oui, Mademoiselle.*"

Simon looked up from his magazine and in his odd detached way told Christa about the two deer they had seen. "I'm going to e-mail dad about the deer. Maybe he'll hire a game warden to..."

Christa closed the boy's magazine and said, "Tomorrow, Simon. As soon as you finish your ice cream, it's upstairs to brush you teeth and go to bed. And, no computer."

He looked at Tim and asked, "Do I have to?"

"She's the boss. Come on. Upstairs. I'll go with you."

He took Simon's spoon and helped himself to a taste of ice cream. The boy started to protest, but Tim silenced him by feeding Simon the last bite. Liking the playful attention, he left the kitchen. As Tim followed, Christa called after him, "Make sure he brushes his teeth."

Belle leaned against the dishwasher, took a long pull at the beer bottle and said, "That Tim, he's a natural father."

"The dishes, Belle."

@

In Simon's cyberspace domain the boy was already absorbed by the colorful, flashing images on the monitor. His small, stubby hands worked a computer game joy-stick manipulating two crudely animated figures on the large screen. In flashing color pixels by the millions, Tim watched the cartoon-like outline of a grotesquely muscled wrestler dragging a hag of a woman toward a burning pyre. She wasn't Joan of Arc. He looked closer and saw that Crusher's face had been altered. He was younger and had Simon's facial characteristics.

Tim shifted focus to the woman and saw she resembled Christa. Before Simon directed the Crusher to hurl his victim onto the flames Tim said, "Hold it a moment. Isn't that your face and Christa's on those characters?"

The boy turned to Tim and said, "Dad taught me how to scan photos and put them on my game people. Really cool, right?"

"Your dad's pretty smart, isn't he?"

"He thinks so."

Simon turned his attention to the screen and furiously worked the joystick. In jerky stop-motion the wrestler hurled the Christa character into the flames and the screen went dark.

"What's next?"

"That's as far as I've got, but it's going to be a neat game when it's done. She's a witch and..."

Behind them, Christa stood in the doorway and her cold voice intruded, "I may be a witch, Simon, but this one's only doing her job. Time to shut down. Right, Tim?"

Tim reached for the switch, but before he could cut the power Simon knocked his hand away. "Hey, I got to save first. Don't you know anything? And, besides I just let it run."

"After you tuck boy wonder into bed, I'll see you in the kitchen."

CHAPTER NINE

Christa paced the kitchen's industrial red tile floor glaring coldly at Tim. Belle watched them and fought to hold back her desire to come to the young man's defense. Then Christa paused to go eyeball to eyeball with Tim. "He couldn't wait to get back to his computer. And you let him. Starting tomorrow, and for the next ten days, you are going to give him a real life."

"He'll need a lot more time than that to withdraw from cyberspace."

"For some reason, which I can't fathom, Simon worships you. You were hired to get that boy away from his computer and help him lose some weight. Do so, or pack up and move on."

Belle had heard enough. She stepped between them, "That boy's mother and father, they're always too busy for him. I do not dare tell them, but that damn computer is giving him what they are not giving him. And it's so real it makes me seasick to watch it. You should see the rivers of blood and blown apart bodies he watches. And, nobody really hugs him, or listens to him but me, and that's a fact."

Christa nodded agreeing with the younger woman and turned back to Tim. "Tomorrow, it's cold turkey for Simon. So get off your nice guy high horse and take charge of that boy. And no more ice cream for him either."

At the top of the staircase Simon heard Christa hurling orders at Tim. He couldn't stand the sound of her shrill attack on his friend and went back to his room. At the computer he worked the joy-stick and again Crusher Simon flung Christa Hag into the blazing pyre.

Early the next morning Tim was on the dock searching for the leak in the canoe. He quickly found where the canvas that had been laid over the strip cedar hull decades ago had been punctured. It would be an easy fix. As he started for the boathouse to gather tools he heard Simon calling for him, "Tim, I made the posters!"

He turned to see Simon running along the dock waving a hand full of red card stock. The boy's unusual enthusiasm caused Tim to grin. Simon held a poster up in front of Tim's eyes and demanded, "What do you think?"

NO HUNTING
PRIVATE PROPERTY
VIOLATORS WILL BE
PERSECUTED!

Tim smiled at Simon's misuse of the word, but, knowing the kid as he did, Tim figured he had picked the right warning. Yeah, Simon would want them persecuted.

Around the bold type Simon had printed several skulls and crossbones. There was no doubt that the boy was dead serious about the no hunting sign project. As Simon lowered the poster Tim said, "Nice touch, those skulls and crossbones, but what happens if we find some hunters?"

Simon's response came out with rapid enthusiasm. "We radio for the state fish and game wardens, then we call Friday Harbor Security. Dad hired them to watch the place, so they have to come if we call. They're only half an hour away by fast boat, and they've got a fast one. If the game wardens or security catch them, bam! They go to jail. Then we can sue 'em for trespass, too. How many posters will we need?"

"Let's start with a couple dozen. And we'll make a picnic of it. I'll ask Belle to pack us lunch."

"Can she come with us?"

"Sure. Why not?"

Simon considered Tim's question as if it needed an answer and said, "No reason I can think of. She's fun."

"Then you invite her."

The boy smiled faintly, nodded okay, and turned to run back down the dock.

An hour later Tim, Simon and Belle walked out of the kitchen with day packs slung on their backs. As they passed Christa, who was sitting in the sun working the keys of her laptop, she gave them a half-hearted wave. Only Tim returned her gesture. When they reached the beach he paused to look back at the woman. "Hey, I bet she's lonely..."

He retraced his steps and Simon watched him approach Christa. When Tim closed the top of her computer and pointed toward shore the boy scowled. Then he saw the woman shake her head in refusal and indicate a stack of papers on the patio table. With a shrug, Tim ran back to join them. Simon felt a glow of pleasure and found that he was actually looking

71

forward to entering the dense, damp island forest again.

Beyond the rocky headland, a few yards from shore where a short stretch of cobble beach would allow a boat to land at high tide they tacked the first "NO HUNTING" poster to a tree where the warning would be seen from the water. Simon stood back to admire the sign. "I'd pay attention to that, wouldn't you, Tim?"

"It would depend on how badly I wanted a deer," he replied seriously.

Simon sensed the emotional weight in Tim's voice. He was about to ask him what he really meant, but Belle interrupted by saying, "I wouldn't hunt here if I saw that sign."

They continued around the island tacking no hunting signs where hunters might land a boat until they ran out of posters.

"Let's explore inland," said Tim. "There's more than four square miles here. No telling what we'll find."

Simon looked to Belle for reassurance. She nodded her okay and the boy felt better. They turned away from the shore and began climbing upward, finding the way easier along small streams that trickled down from the island's single, high hill. Surprisingly, the thick stand of cedars began to thin and they came upon a clearing where they found the small lake that caught the runoff from the upper slopes. As they climbed over the thick trunk of a fallen tree and began circling the lake Tim observed, "Really strange, a lake within an island."

Tim moved closer to the rocky edge and peered into the clear water. Movement below the surface caught his attention. With surprise Tim exclaimed, "Look, there's salmon in there, wild Chinook salmon! Dozens of 'em. They're spawning right up here. Amazing."

Tim kept staring into the water as if the reddish, hook-nosed males and the egg swollen big-bellied females were some sort of heaven sent creation. "There's hardly a wild run left in these parts. Most of the salmon are hatchery raised. But these guys, I bet they've still got their natural genes. Simon, you have a treasure here, a real biological treasure. Now, my young friend, you have a purpose in life."

"What's that, Tim?"

"Making sure this salmon run continues. Your father, and I'm sure he knows it, has become caretaker of one of the last wild salmon runs in the San Juan Islands. And I kid you not, it's a big deal. Maybe more of a big deal than what he's doing in Holland."

Simon was puzzled by Tim's outburst of enthusiasm for the salmon. He knew that several of the north coast salmon groups had recently been placed on the Endangered Species List, and that the catch had been declining for many years. He told himself, "I'll check it out on the web. Now do I type in salmon or endangered species? Or maybe there's a dot org like 'Save the Salmon'. And how come Tim wants to catch one if they're that endangered?"

A quarter mile beyond the far side of the lake, where virgin forest again dominated the landscape, their path was blocked by a deep gorge that captured the lake's overflow and sent the water tumbling swiftly downward along the narrow river to the strait. Stopped by the ravine, Tim opened his backpack and brought out the Nikon. "Let's get a few pictures of this for your mom and dad."

As he opened the camera's leather case, Simon moved to peer into the steep water filled gorge, hoping to see a salmon fighting its way upward to the lake. By his feet a giant cedar had fallen across the gap, forming a precarious bridge to the far side of the chasm. Without thinking the boy stepped onto the wet moss-slick log and started across. His arms were outstretched like a tightrope walker and a few feet from the bank he looked down at the cascading river far below and began to experience vertigo. Simon froze.

When Belle sensed that Simon was not by her side she turned to look for him. What she saw brought a gasp. Simon was beginning to sway and looked like he might tumble into the deep gorge any second. Belle fought down panic. She didn't want to alarm the obviously frightened child and called softly to Tim. "Simon needs help. Best you get him right now."

Tim looked up from his camera and saw the boy losing his balance. Moving quickly, he walked out onto the fallen log and grabbed Simon. He felt the spongy, rotten wood start to give way under their combined weight. Without a pause he back stepped off the log, drawing them both to safety.

Belle took Simon into her arms and held the trembling boy against her heart. "*Mon dieu*, little man. You gave us a scare."

Tim crouched before Simon and, like Alex laying down the law, he peered into his eyes. "That log is rotted right through. If it had snapped from our weight, down we'd go, and good-bye Simon and Tim."

Simon twisted from Belle's arms and moved to look into the gorge. He saw that Tim was right. Nobody could escape the racing torrent of water that blasted down the rock strewn crevice. Tim drew him back from the edge and said, "In this country, everything that lies on the ground, unless it's rock or cement, is going to rot. So, guys, we'd better watch it."

"This is getting dangerous, Tim. I think we've come far enough," said Belle with a note of foreboding.

As if Simon were not a part of the conservation, Tim answered Belle, "If he never faces danger, how can he deal with the real world, or feel fear and love?"

They started back, looking for a place to picnic along the shore where the sun would warm them. As they followed a small stream down the slope Tim abruptly stopped and crouched to examine the ground. Simon and Belle watched him trace the outline of an animal track deeply imprinted in the damp soil. He touched its sharply defined claw marks, then whispered in awe, "Bear track, a really big one."

He indicated where the spongy moss had been crushed by the weight of the bear's giant paw. They could see that the depression was slowly filling with brackish water. "He's close, probably came by here minutes ago looking for salmon, or berries, or both."

As Belle watched, Simon put his own foot in the paw print and saw there was room for both feet. Clearly, it was a big bear. The boy and the woman looked to Tim for reassurance and he motioned for them to back away from the area. As they cautiously moved off Simon turned to Tim to ask a question. He silenced the boy by putting a finger to his lips and shook his head. They moved on, arrived at one of the island's few clearings, and started across. They all saw the bear at the same time and froze.

Thirty yards away, on the far side of the small meadow, a very large male black bear was feeding on tops of fiddle ferns, seemingly unconcerned about the intruders into his world. They watched him delicately bite off the green spiral tips of the ferns. Then the breeze carried their scent toward the big bear. He stopped foraging and lifted his nose to sniff. Despite the bear's poor eyesight it immediately sensed them and stood tall to look their way. All seven feet and four hundred pounds of the big black said that he was a powerful predator, and in an instant could kill them all with the swipe of a paw.

Tim slowly drew Bell and Simon against him into a tight group and

75

began to lead them away from the bear. As they backed off he began speaking in a soft soothing voice, "Its okay, bear. We're leaving. Relax bear. We'll be gone in a minute. Just be a nice bear..."

Still facing the humans, the bear dropped to his four feet. Sure he would charge, Simon held his breath. Belle fought down a desire to run and looked at Tim wanting to know what to do next.

As they backed off Simon could feel Tim's tension easing, but he saw that Belle was wide-eyed with fear. Then Tim spoke in the same soft reassuring way, "We're going big boy. Bye-bye bear."

"Stick close guys. We look bigger that way. And, bears can sense when you don't mean them any harm."

"Can we run now?" asked Belle.

"You run, you're prey, and he's going to get you."

"How about climbing a tree?" Simon asked.

"Not with black bears. They climb like monkeys," cautioned Tim. "With grizzlies, that would be okay. They don't climb trees."

When the bear returned to feeding, they collectively gave a sigh of relief. With a final glance at the animal Belle took a breath and said, "*Mon dieu. Tres formidable*. He is huge."

"And fast. Bears have been clocked running thirty-five miles an hour. Grizzlies have been filmed taking down a running moose."

"And next we'll run into a moose," teased Belle.

@

Back at the beach they sat on a driftwood log and unwrapped ham and Swiss cheese sandwiches Belle made. She was still excited about the bear encounter and said, "That bear was something to write home about, if I still had a home there."

"Do you miss Haiti?" asked Tim.

"Yes, very much, but I can't go back. My father was political. He was always on the losing side. Always far left of center. After the right wing took over, the police arrested him. But the earthquake flattened the prison and he escaped. I've heard from him only once since then. He sent a postcard that was mailed from Mexico saying he was well. If I returned to Haiti they would take me hostage to lure my father back and punish him. Please, keep this to yourself, Tim."

Wanting to be included Simon added, "Tell Tim about the cockroaches!"

Belle gave the boy a withering glare. "Another time, Simon."

Tim put his arm around Belle to comfort her. Simon felt left out. He moved closer to Tim and asked, "Would that bear have eaten us?"

"Not likely. There's salmon in the creek and plenty of berries and ferns."

"He shouldn't be here. It's not his island."

Tim laid a hand on the boy's shoulder, "When you saw that bear, did you ever feel more alive?"

Not sure what Tim was getting at, Simon waited for him to continue.

"Without that bear, the deer, and the salmon this island is nothing but rocks, a big house, and a lot of really special trees."

"You certainly were fired up by Mister Bear," observed Belle.

"I like their power. Here they dominate. When you meet one close up its life or death, and no bullshit. Kind of like big business, isn't it?"

Not waiting for an answer, Tim stood and turned to face the water, cutting off further conversation, "Time to get back."

CHAPTER TEN

Mouth agape in a state of mild shock, Christa listened as Simon described their encounter with the bear who grew more ferocious with the boy's telling. Belle was pleased with the impact of his highly dramatic tale on the Yankee woman. Tim fought to suppress a laugh as Simon recalled with unusual enthusiasm, "…and then he turned to glare at us and started to charge. But Tim, he told that bear we were friendly and…"

"You could all have been mauled, or worse," Christa said. You remember what happened to that young man, and his name was Tim too, and his girlfriend in Alaska. They were both eaten."

Turning to Tim she scolded, "Really, you're carrying this outdoor adventure experience a bit far."

"Tim likes bears," Belle explained, "And that one seemed to like him. I speak God's truth."

"I must insist Tim that you act more responsibly."

"Okay, Christa. We'll stay away from bears. But Belle here, she wants to see a moose. If you'd like to join us tomorrow for moose watching."

Christa had had enough of their teasing and turned to leave. At the doorway, she fired a verbal parting shot, "Grow up, Tim."

Despite himself, Simon giggled.

When Simon had been put to bed without protesting, and Christa was working upstairs, Tim invited Belle to join him on the patio. Under a full moon they gazed at the sparkling, still water. A touch of damp fall chill was in the air and they both wore sweaters. From the patio stereo speakers came the melancholy voice of the famous Portuguese fado singer, Amalia Rodriguez.

Belle had selected the tape and explained, "Though not in my language, Amalia's voice speaks out to all exiles. She's singing about lost love and a country far away. This one was recorded when Portugal was still a dictatorship and had African colonies. Amalia was the voice of the poor. She learned her songs from Lisbon's blind beggars and widows of fishermen lost at sea. Later she sang of soldiers who died in the African wars."

"Her songs touched you," Tim whispered.

"Deeply."

They stared across the shimmering inlet and neither spoke until Tim said, "It's beautiful, but not like the tropics. You must miss Haiti."

"What I miss are my family, warm nights and my language."

He stood and reached out for her hand. "Dance with me, Belle."

"With pleasure, *Mon Cherie*."

He drew Belle against him and they began to slowly dance in time with the fado singer's plaintive, sexual voice.

From his upstairs bedroom Simon watched the couple. After a moment he closed the paned glass window and drew the curtain.

From the couch, Simon peered at the monitor and worked the computer game joystick. On the screen The Crusher was embracing

80

a chocolate-skinned, bare breasted woman. The wrestler's face now resembled Simon's, and the woman recently scanned into Simon's game was Belle.

@

An hour after dawn Bell's worried voice woke Tim, "Karl's boat's gone and he didn't take the breakfast I left out for him."

Tim shook off the fog of sleep, "The gardener?"

"He's never left before without taking food for his boat."

"Maybe he's gone fishing. The salmon are running."

"It's his leaky old dory I'm worried about. It's as ancient as Karl."

Tim rolled out of bed and pulled on shorts. "Okay. I'll look for him, after coffee and something to eat. And I'll take Simon and he can catch a salmon today."

Tim was pleasantly surprised that Simon agreed to sail with him aboard Alex's 22-foot sloop. Simon had bought Tim's appeal to combine a hunt for the gardener with a sailing lesson and trolling a lure for a Chinook. As Tim put the sloop on a heading for the main channel he asked the boy what he knew about the old man. Simon shrugged, "The only person he was friendly with was Dad. And I think he was pissed off because he had to give up his place so you could move into the boathouse."

"There's no reason he should be mad at me, I never even met the old guy."

"He's always moody, but Dad says he's a great sailor. He sails his old dory all over these islands."

Tim brought binoculars to his eyes and scanned the coastline. "The weather's good. Hell, he could have sailed anywhere. Let's give it a couple

81

of hours. Then we'll head back and fish on the way home."

"Then what, Tim?"

"If we don't hear from him by tomorrow we'll call Coast Guard and report him missing."

"Shouldn't we do that sooner?"

Simon's keeper shook his head, "On this sloop I'm captain, and your are first mate, so you follow my orders. Now, bring the fishing rod and tackle box out of the dock locker. Got that, Simon?"

"Got it, Captain."

By eleven Tim gave up the search and put the sloop on a heading for Greenlee's inlet. He tied a silver spinner to a leader fastened to a fishing line. Tim let the lure unroll from the reel and they began trolling for a salmon. As the sloop cruised along in a light breeze he began explaining the basics of fishing, "It's all about putting the lure or a baited hook where the fish are. And I think they're right about where we're trolling. They see the flashing silver or feel its vibration and think it's a free dinner. But fish are smart, so fishers like us have to be smarter. If we weren't trolling a lure we'd be jiggling a baited hook. And a smart fish would nudge the bait and we'd feel the line move. Then what, Simon?"

"We'd reel in the line a bit to make the fish think the bait was escaping, and then it'd bite. Like the lure of advertising, right Tim?"

"Crusher did that to get you to buy his poster."

Simon nodded thoughtfully and was about to comment when something struck the lure and an instant later, took the hook. The tip of the rod bent downward. Tim secured the tiller, moved beside Simon, and in a calm voice coached him, "You've got one. Tighten the drag first, then give the rod a sharp pull to set the hook."

Simon yanked on the rod with all his strength.

"Good job, Simon. Now begin reeling in slowly. If he takes a rest and there's slack in the line, reel it in as fast as your can. If he makes a run for it, give him some slack so he won't snap the line."

He watched the boy fight the unseen fish. It was a big one. In five minutes Simon's arms and hands would cry out with pain. Would he have the toughs to reel the fish in? Tim reached for the sharp pointed gaff in readiness to bring the catch aboard. As the fish surfaced it made a final lunge trying to throw the hook from its jaw. The Chinook's struggle impressed Tim and he mused, "You're right, Simon. That spinning lure is kind of like an advertisement. In this case he bought the message and he's our dinner." Louder now, he encouraged Simon, "You're doing fine, very slowly now, bring him alongside."

The gaff flashed in the bright sunlight and the sharp point buried itself in the fish just behind its gills, "Got him!" Tim yelled happily. "You're a fisherman now, Simon."

Tim drew the salmon aboard and Tim walked Simon through the process of bleeding, gutting, and preparing the Chinook for cooking. The boy worked the filleting knife with detached interest as a surgeon might. Simon slid the guts overboard and remarked, "Yep, Tim. Catching a fish is a metaphor for taking advantage of someone."

Tim gave Simon a questioning glance and remembered him saying, "Kids know everything."

A mile off the dock, where the water calmed, they cruised serenely across the broad inlet. Tim had the Jennifer on a broad reach and she sailed smoothly downwind. As he held the tiller he explained a few of the finer points of sailing to Simon. "In the inlet here, the winds are always variable..."

"Because the landmass of the island disturbs the normal flow, right?"

"You're catching on fast."

Tim moved aside to make room for Simon at the helm. Without giving him a chance to become anxious, he casually slid aside and Simon grabbed the tiller. "Okay, Simon, take us home."

The boy obeyed without question and the fresh breeze sped the sloop along swiftly. Simon had unconsciously absorbed the simple concept that air passing over the convex side of the sail created a low pressure area, as does an airplane wing. The higher pressure, on the other side of the sail, creates the force needed to propel the boat.

Tim pointed to the nearby headland and coached him through the basics of tacking back and forth on a windward course so they could arrive at a certain spot. The boy quickly picked up the skill and they reached the rocky point of land.

Simon was feeling increasingly confident and his mind quickly computed the angle of the wind and how much the bow should be pointed off the wind to achieve the desired angle of attack. With Tim handling the lines, they turned back for the island on a downwind reach. As they neared the dock, and a collision seemed possible, Simon began to grow anxious and looked to Tim for instruction.

"You're doing great, Simon. When we near the dock, I'll take over. And since we're sailing downwind, I'm going to have to jibe to come about."

"Jibe?"

"Means the stern has got to cross the eye of the wind and the sail's boom is going to swing across the cockpit really hard... like slamming a door shut. So, when I yell 'jibe ho' you duck!" He took the tiller from the boy and judged their distance from the dock. They were closing fast. Tim let out the main sheet, pulled the tiller in hard and yelled, "Jibe-ho!" The boom swung violently across the cockpit and Simon ducked just in time avoid being struck. The bow turned into the wind and Tim steered the sloop alongside the dock and dropped the sail. Simon jumped out to secure the dock lines and shouted, "That was cool!"

"You'll be jibing tomorrow."

"Yes!"

CHAPTER ELEVEN

A roaring whomp-whomping sound blasted them and they looked skyward. A Bell Ranger helicopter was descending for the estate's wide front lawn. As the chopper passed over the dock its rotor's downwash almost blew them into the water.

Simon saw Tim's look of concern and then noticed the letters painted on the helicopter's fuselage. "What's INS mean, Tim?"

"Immigration and Naturalization Service. What the hell are they doing out here?"

They ran along the dock and up the flagstone path to the lawn and arrived as the helicopter touched down on the grass. Two men in suits jumped out followed by two others dressed in black military tactical assault gear. Simon saw that the uniformed soldiers were carrying automatic rifles. He tried to comprehend what was happening and what danger might come, but all he could think of was that they were after his father for something he did. Then he saw the two armed men split up and trot around separate sides of the house. Simon glanced fearfully at Tim and tugged on his shirt. "What do they want?"

"Let's find out. We have nothing to hide."

Simon kept close to Tim and the men in suits moved swiftly for them. Their jackets were open and Simon saw that they had hand guns in holsters under their coats. He went wide-eyed with dread as he realized this weird happening wasn't a computer game.

"Do you live here?" snapped the taller of the two men.

"I work here," said Tim matching the man's official tone.

Simon heard the shorter one, who had a crew cut, a deep tan, and looked like a character out of his "Nazi Tank Attack" computer game demand, "Do you know a Belle Dubois?"

"Sure, she works here. What's the big deal?"

The tall agent spoke next, "We'd like to talk with her."

"We do have a phone," said Tim not being nice.

"Don't get smart," threatened the shorter man.

Then Belle's frightened voice, sounding louder than Simon had ever heard, turned their attention to the house. "Tim, don't let them take me away!"

The two armed men in battle dress held Belle by the arms and were dragging her across the lawn for the helicopter. She fought to escape and kicked at their legs.

Then Christa sprinted out of the house and charged in front of Belle and the armed men, blocking their way. She demanded furiously, "Would someone tell me what the hell is going on here?"

When the armed men side-stepped around her and forced Belle toward the helicopter Christa turned on the two in suits, "What right do you have to swoop down here on private property and abduct that young woman?"

The taller agent pulled a folded document from his inside jacket pocket and thrust it at Christa. "This is a legal Immigration and Naturalization Service deportation warrant, signed by a Federal Judge."

Christa snatched it from his hand and briefly scanned the document. "Nevertheless, there's been some kind of terrible bureaucratic screw up. If you take her away I'm going with you and sort his matter out."

"Lady, this is official business. So, back off, or I'll cite you for obstructing a Federal Officer."

Her voice grew stronger. "Your superiors will hear from the Greenlee family attorney before the day is out and he'll have your ass."

"Cool it, lady," the short agent ordered. "If Mister Greenlee wants to make a case of this, tell him that employing an illegal alien is a serious offense. And if Greenlee hasn't paid her Social Security, IRS will have his ass."

Christa backed off.. Before she could speak again, the helicopter's engine roared and the wind from the rotor blades blasted them. Over the loud noise they heard Belle's final cry, "Please do something!"

Simon darted from Tim and the others on a frantic dash for Belle. Before the boy could reach the terrified woman the armed men hurled her into the helicopter. The men in suits turned to climb aboard. Tim stopped the taller one and Simon heard him say calmly, "She's family. They have a right to know what happened."

He thought for a moment and explained, "We received an anonymous e-mail about her. We ran a computer check and found she's wanted for anti-government terrorist activities in Haiti."

Tim muttered, "And Homeland Security wins another..."

The man stiffened, "Watch what you say, Mister."

Then the tall agent climbed aboard slammed the cabin door. The helicopter lifted off the lawn. As the downwash battered Simon he looked up and saw Belle's face in the cabin window. Tears were streaming down her cheeks. Now numb with shock, Simon could only stare at the rising thunderous machine that was taking Belle out of his life.

CHAPTER TWELVE

Since the shock of Belle's abduction the day before, only the computer and the monitor's glowing images held Simon's interest. He sought emotional solace in his cyberspace world and refused to talk about her. Tim and Christa, hard as they tried, couldn't separate the boy from his computer. Even the news that Christa had e-mailed the Greenlees about Belle and that Alex had responded immediately saying he would use all of his connections to get Belle back, failed to lift the boy's gloom. Then he refused to eat. Christa's hamburgers and Tim's omelets wouldn't do. He even shook his head when offered ice cream. Saying he wanted Belle's cooking, Simon headed upstairs to his computer.

Christa considered calling the Greenlees and asking them to return. Tim urged her to wait another day. He suggested it wouldn't hurt Simon to lose a couple of pounds and went upstairs to spend some quality time with him.

Simon didn't acknowledge Tim's arrival. He continued to work the joystick in a game of life and death where only the strong and mindless survive. BAD WORLD had totally captivated Simon. He was Jack, a fighting machine battling his way out of a trap the Death Watch terrorists had set to kill this half-man half-motorcycle cyberhero.

Tim saw that Simon had mastered the use of the ultra violent game's fantastic weapons. The dark room and the black and white images on the screen, helped highlight splashes of gory red blood gushing from dismembered arms and legs. The beat up and kill game held Simon like a steel wolf trap. With intense concentration the boy battled outlandish foes that melted from blasts of futuristic flame throwers shot by super-muscled, garishly costumed avatars. When Simon had torched the last evildoer, and his final score was extremely high, the computer announced, "Congratulations. You have been promoted to BAD WORLD Exterminator Captain."

Tim's laughter snapped Simon back to the reality of his room and he spun to stare at him.

"Really, Simon. That one's so over the top it's funny. I've never seen anything that brutal and blood-drenched. When you throw a guy like a dart and his head gets buried in a cork bulls eye, well that's close to warped sick genius. How can you look at it any other way?"

Simon got it and began to giggle. "How come, Tim, you know about BAD WORLD?

"One of the older campers smuggled in a game and console. Before I confiscated it we played BAD WORLD. Then I locked it up until camp ended."

Simon really laughed at that, "Tim that is s-o-o-o not cool."

Then the boy's mood abruptly changed. In a harsh voice of outraged injustice he accused, "Christa did it."

"Did what?"

"Sent those INS guys a poison pen e-mail about Belle. It's easy.

Anybody could do it. Even you. And since her father's on some sort of FBI, CIA, watch list, or Homeland Security no-fly-list, or maybe all three, they'd pay attention."

Tim shook his head, "Why would Christa do a terrible thing like that."

The boy moved closer and whispered, as if Christa might be listening, "She likes you and she was jealous of Belle. I hate her."

Come on, Simon. You've seen the way she treats me."

Instead of arguing, Simon logged onto a web browser and brought up a site. "See what I found? The FBI e-mail address. Suppose I told them that Christa was a spy or a terrorist or something and signed it 'A Patriotic American'. They'd come after her."

"I'd rather you wouldn't. And besides, Christa's your father's business partner."

"Junior partner. She sucks."

"Christa's just lonely. This isn't her thing out here. Have a heart, Simon. And remember, the first thing she did was to call your father's lawyer. And then she called her Congressman. And your father's on the case. They'll get her back."

"I bet they already have Belle on a plane to Haiti. They'll put her in prison, or what's left of one. There won't be another earthquake so Belle can escape like her father did. She'll die there or they'll torture her and then kill her."

Tim was surprised by Simon's unexpected outburst. He stood and placed his hands on the boy's shoulders. "Stuff happens, Simon. The lawyers and politicians will handle it. Log off and let's go sailing."

The boy shook his head. Tim spoke softly, "Christa's gonna fire me if I don't do my job."

"And your job is to keep me away from the computer."

Simon stood and said, "Maybe I'll send a poison pen e-mail to Internal Revenue Service about Christa cheating on her income tax."

Tim liked that idea. He suppressed a laugh, and pulled Simon from the chair. "That's going too far. Well, maybe later. Enough for now. Let's go sailing"

@

As Tim and Simon rigged the little sloop for a sail Christa walked out onto the dock. She was lonely and depressed. It was Sunday and no one was at the office to receive her faxes and e-mails. There would be no news, good or otherwise, from Alex either. Tim listened to her frustration and tried to console her, "Perhaps tomorrow they'll sign the deal."

"God, I hope so. This waiting is giving me an ulcer."

She stepped back to watch the man and the boy checking the boat's rigging and noticed that Simon's glum mood seemed to have lightened. She glanced at the inlet, noted the light breeze that hardly ruffled the water. Despite Simon's angry glare at her, she softly murmured, "Tim, make sure Simon wears a life jacket."

"We always do," Tim said evenly. With a smile he added, "There's one for you, if you'd care to join us."

"No thank you. I'm not a water person."

Simon murmured to Tim, "I bet she can't even swim."

He ignored the boy and gave the stern woman a warm, inviting smile. "Not much wind today. We'll just be cruising around slow and easy. You might enjoy it."

"Perhaps tomorrow."

"We'll plan on tomorrow then."

He shoved the sloop away from the dock and jumped aboard, then pushed out the sail's boom to catch the wind. They were off and he surrendered the tiller to Simon. When the boy had the boat on a heading for open water Tim said, "A couple times sailing with us just might defrost her."

"You like her, don't you?"

"It's more like I feel sorry for her. All her brains and she's got no one who cares for her."

"She's a bitch nerd who works for my father."

"What's wrong with being a nerd? They've changed the world. And how about you? You're a cyberspace freak."

"But I like going sailing with you."

Tim laughed long and hard until Simon interrupted, "And maybe we'll spot old Karl stranded on an island eating clams."

Tim's laughter stopped abruptly. "Oh, shit. With all that happened to Belle I forgot to call the Coast Guard. If he's not back by dark, I'll report him missing."

As Christa left the dock she heard Tim's distant laughter stop. She turned to stare at the sloop. Then with a sigh she walked to the empty house thinking that tomorrow she would overcome her fears and go sailing with them.

After sailing, Tim coaxed Simon away from his computer by picking up the boy's small bow and insisting they go outside to fire a few arrows. Simon reluctantly shut down and followed Tim to the back yard.

To the rear of the main house, near the greenhouse where Simon's mother and Belle raised flowers and vegetables, the boy's father had set up four bales of straw for an archery backstop. Fixed to the straw was a conventional bull's eye target with one exception. On the bull's eye itself was a photo of Mr. Microsoft himself, Bill Gates. Alex's fellow cyberbaron and principal competitor was smiling benevolently at all who cared to look.

Simon's first arrow hit a few inches to the left of Mr. Gates' ear. Tim laughed and said, "My turn."

They were shooting Simon's small bow; the one his dad had bought for him to use at summer camp. Though it had only a forty pound pull, it was finely crafted of English yew. If the archer was skilled, and his aim true, the steel-tipped target arrow would find its mark up to a distance of one hundred feet.

Tim shot next. His arrow struck a foot over Gates' head. Simon grabbed the bow, notched an arrow to the string and pulled it back as far as he could. He sighted on the target's nose, made a slight correction for the breeze, and let fly. TWANG! The arrow missed Gate's nose, but pierced his chin.

"You're doing better than at camp."

"No one's forcing me to be in a contest."

From behind them Christa called out, "Good shot, Simon."

They turned to see her watching them. She was smiling hesitantly. Simon saw Tim wave at her to join them and muttered in his annoyed squeaky voice, "Bitch nerd."

"Enough of that, Simon," Tim warned.

When Christa joined them, the boy gave her stink-eye, but Tim offered her the bow. "Care to shoot a few?"

"If I'm not intruding."

Tim's smile said she was welcome and he turned to Simon, "How about collecting the arrows?"

The boy scowled at Christa and turned to walk off to the target. Tim gestured to the bow and remarked, "It's really a kid's bow, but it draws well."

She checked the bow for warp, gave the string a pull and said, "Only a forty pound pull. Nicely made, though."

Tim saw she had some familiarity with archery and said, "The target's at a hundred feet. If you'd care to move closer..."

"Not unless it's too far away for you."

He glanced quizzically at Christa.

Simon returned with a handful of arrows and dropped them into a wire quiver that had been driven into the damp spongy lawn. With an annoyed look at Tim he walked off to the house, resenting his friend's interest in the woman.

Ignoring Simon's rudeness, Christa selected an arrow, checked the shaft for straightness and notched it to the bow string. Tim watched her judge the wind and confidently draw the arrow back. Without hesitating she released the string. Her arrow shot for the target straight and true. The steel point hit the Gates photo right under his thinning hair.

They shot five arrows each and Christa's skill was such that she easily beat Tim. Her last shot punctured Bill's throat. Tim gave her a courtly bow of congratulations and said in a voice reminiscent of Errol Flynn in the old Warner Brother's Robin Hood film, "That was rather splendid, My Lady."

Catching the spirit of his playfulness she lightly countered, "Thank you, My Lord. Shall we move closer for the next round?"

"If it pleases My Lady, but I must concede I have been bested sufficiently for this day. And pray tell where did you learn to send an arrow so true?"

Dropping the act, but still enjoying the lighthearted mood she said, "University of California, Berkeley. It was either archery or swimming."

Remembering what she had said earlier, Tim remarked, "And you're not a water person."

"But I do enjoy walking in the rain."

He laughed lightly and then grew reflective. Moving closer to her he said, "What a world. Here we are in the Twenty-first Century, playing with a ten thousand year old weapon..."

"... in the fortress of a cyberbaron."

"Well said, My Lady.".

For the first time since she had met him, Christa smiled warmly at Tim. Catching herself out of character and yet being drawn to him, she turned from the young man and looked for Simon. She noticed he had disappeared. "Better get to work, Tim. He's you know where."

CHAPTER THIRTEEN

It was social networking tutorial time. Simon and Tim sat on the couch in front of the monitor. Simon, the eleven-year-old instructor, watched his frowning student attempted to bring up the colorful home page of an Internet gamer chat room site. The screen quickly filled with the bold letters of a pop-up ad for a low interest rate Visa credit card. A pretty girl touted a free weekend getaway bag that was yours for taking advantage of this once in a lifetime offer.

"You don't want that. Kill it with a click," said Simon happily playing teacher. Tim glanced at the boy. Had he so quickly forgotten Belle and the old gardener? Had his computer replaced them?

Tim moved the cursor to the "No Thanks" box, obliterated the ad and advised, "You'd better turn on your pop-up blocker."

Simon looked sheepish, "I had to turn it off because I wanted to copyright my video game by e-mail. The copyright office is so specific its pain in the ass, I'm going to snail mail my application when the game's finished."

Seeing the glowing mail box symbol, the boy ordered, "Click that."

There was real e-mail, from The Crusher and the boy's parents. Simon grabbed the mouse from Tim. "Wow, Crusher really answered." On the screen they read:

Hi, Simon Cyberfan,
Thanks a heap for your e-mails. Would have
answered sooner, but I've been on the road. Your
game could be a winner. I'd like to log in with
you and give it a try. I'll let you know what a pro
thinks of it..."

Tim saw Simon frown and the boy began reading aloud, "If I had your password, we could network your PC and play together like a tag team. Let me know what you think. Best wishes, Crusher."

"That was a really personal e-mail for me," the excited boy exclaimed. Then he grew somber, "But he wants my password."

Wanting fatherly advice, Simon looked at Tim and added, "It's just a computer game."

You know about passwords."

"Yeah, I know. You only give it to someone your really trust. "I'll e-mail back I'm thinking about it."

As Simon moved the cursor to reply to Crusher's e-mail he was interrupted by Christa's voice, "Lunch is ready, you guys."

Before the boy could respond to the Crusher Tim said, "Lunch will wait. How about reading your parents' e-mail?"

They learned that all was going well in Holland and that the family attorney and their Congressman had made contact with INS about freeing Belle. They cautioned it might take time, but were confident of success. Alex and Jennifer sent their love to all and would be returning as planned.

After lunch Tim led Simon to the dock and asked the boy to help him repair the old canoe. "We should varnish those weathered cane seats, too."

Tim opened the storage locker attached to the boathouse and brought out tools and sandpaper, fiberglass cloth and resin to patch the hole. As they set to work he ran a hand over the canoe's hull. "This one's a classic. Not many of these old canvas covered wood canoes left."

"Yeah, but you don't have to varnish Fiberglass ones."

@

The booming report of a high powered rifle coming from the island's interior caused them to look toward the woods. Tim muttered what-the-hell and said, "Rifle shot. High caliber!"

Working at the computer in her room, Christa also heard the loud rifle crack. Startled, she stood and moved to look out the window. What she saw caused her to swear and she grabbed binoculars from a bookshelf. She brought the field glasses to her eyes, adjusted the focus and zeroed in on the shore beyond the rocky headland. From her second story elevation she saw two hunters dragging a male deer toward an inflatable outboard motor powered Zodiac beached on the cobbled shore. They had rifles slung over their backs. Christa muttered angrily, "Those bastards!" Holding the binoculars, she dashed from the room.

She ran for the dock yelling, "Tim! Simon! Poachers! They shot a deer, right beyond the headland."

Out of breath and furious, she reported, "They're loading it into a Zodiac right this minute!"

"They killed one of our deer?" asked Simon in disbelief.

Christa gave him a nod of angry confirmation and the boy scowled.

"We have to report this to Fish and Wildlife," insisted Christa.

Tim was already opening the boathouse tool locker. He pulled out a hand-held marine VHF transmitter that sat in a battery charger beside the larger longer range fix-mounted VHF radio. "Report, hell. We're going after those guys."

"Let's take dad's speedboat. It's really fast," urged Simon.

Tim crouched before Simon and spoke carefully, "We can't reach Fish and Wildlife with the hand-held. I'll have to follow them and radio you where they're heading. Your job will be to relay my transmission to the game wardens. Use Channel Sixteen. You know how to use the VHF and what to tell Fish and Game. Christa doesn't. So it has to be you."

"I want to go with you."

"You'll do the most good right here."

He turned to Christa and urgently said, "I'll need your help. Let's go!"

Before Christa had a chance to protest, Tim had the door to the boathouse open and shoved her inside. Alone on the dock Simon felt abandoned, but he did as Tim ordered and turned the VHF radio on, then set the channel selector to sixteen.

Inside the dark boathouse Christa felt a stab of fear constrict her stomach. Tim flicked the light switch. The bright fluorescent tubes revealed a perfectly restored 1950s mahogany 25 foot Chris-Craft open cockpit speedboat.

The boat gleamed with shining chrome and bronze and a fortune lavished on her restoration. In the adjoining slip was the Alaska skiff Tim had arrived aboard. Tim admired Alex Greenlee's toys for the briefest moment and then barked at Christa, "Open the doors and free the dock

102

lines while I start this beauty."

"Tim, I don't think I can…"

"You can do any damn thing you really want to. Come on, Christa. Open those doors!"

His direct commanding voice overcame Christa's uncertainty. There was something in his harsh tone that seemed to come from another very different person. Her reasoning calculating self wanted to examine this surprising perception. She turned to look at Tim and saw his intensity. There was no way Christa could back out.

She hurried along the slip's walkway to the electric powered garage-like roll up doors and flipped the switch. The doors clattered upward on metal tracks and blinding sunlight flooded the boathouse. She returned to the speedboat and freed the dock lines. As they came loose Christa was suddenly conscious that her heart was beating rapidly and her hands were trembling. She was about to protest this unexpected call to action when the engine started, rattling the boathouse with its thunderous roar. Tim threw a life jacket into her arms. "Let's go girl!"

She climbed into the Chris-Craft's cockpit and slid onto the padded red imitation leather seat. Finding no safety belt her anxiety grew. She started to ask Tim where it was, but the engine's scream silenced her. Pushing the throttle full forward, Tim sent the Chris-Craft charging out of the boathouse and into the glaring sunlight.

In an instant they were blasting across the inlet at thirty knots on a course for the distant headland. The hull pounded so hard over the chop that Christa grabbed a handhold to keep from being pitched overboard. Her hair, flying wild, whipped against her cheeks. Despite her fear, this sudden thrust into Tim's daring escapade brought a surge of adrenaline that hyper-charged her body, "My God, is this actually happening to me?"

She glanced back at the dock and saw Simon bringing the shore radio microphone to his lips. He had obeyed Tim again. Then they were racing around the rocky headland. In open water the pounding of the hull grew harder and they were drenched by spray flying over the bow.

Christa raised the binoculars and, despite the boat's jarring vibration, she quickly spotted the two poachers in the Zodiac. "There they are," she shouted over the engine's roar, "I can see the deer's head. It's got antlers." The men in the inflatable hadn't seen them and were moving just fast enough to keep the boat's hull on plane. She clutched Tim's arm and pointed in their direction. He nodded, gave her a wide grin, and whooped, "We got 'em now!"

She liked the way Tim said "we". Gripping the wheel, Tim raised his head over the windshield to see better. To Christa, he did look like some Viking of old on a raid to pillage an Irish village.

He put the hand-held radio mike to his lips and spoke carefully so he would be understood over the speedboat's roar. "Simon, tell Fish and Wildlife they're on a northwest heading, probably for Keller Island..."

"Got it, Tim. What kind of boat?"

He thought, "That kid's really sharp," and radioed Simon a description of the Zodiac.

They raced on and the men they were chasing still seemed oblivious to the pursuing Chris-Craft. As the distance between the two boats narrowed to a quarter of a mile the Zodiac driver glanced back and saw them. He gestured to his partner, gave the outboard full-throttle and the inflatable surged ahead. The Christ Craft was faster and Tim gradually narrowed the gap between the two boats.

He glanced ahead of the poachers and sensed they were heading for a rocky, forested island a couple of miles distant. Tim knew Keller Island was connected to another larger island by a bridge. He guessed that the poachers had a vehicle hidden somewhere near a cove where they could beach the inflatable and escape with the deer by road. Then Simon's voice crackled over the VHF hand-held, "Fish and Wildlife have a boat in the area. Where are those guys now, Tim?"

"Heading for the northwest end of Keller Island. They'll be rounding the point in four or five minutes."

"Guess what, Tim?"

"Tell me," he barked impatiently.

"Fish and Wildlife's boat out of Kingston is on the other side of the island."

"Talk about luck. Thanks, Simon."

Ahead of the Chris-Craft the Zodiac driver's partner raised a rifle and pointed it the speedboat. Christa clutched at Tim, who said reassuringly, "They're bluffing. Don't sweat it."

"How can you be sure?"

"I just know, but in case I'm wrong..."

He backed off on the throttle allowing the inflatable to increase its lead.

The agile Zodiac rounded the island's headland and for a moment it was out of sight. Tim slammed the throttle forward and the Chris-Craft blasted ahead. As they reached Keller Island and passed the point Christa yelled excitedly, "Right into their arms!"

Around the headland surged an immaculate 30 foot Fish and Wildlife patrol boat throwing a white wake off its rakish bow. On the foredeck two uniformed State of Washington Wardens cradled shotguns in their arms, ready for the Zodiac that was on a collision course for the government launch. The driver of the inflatable made a radical turn aside in an attempt to escape.

Before the poachers could evade the patrol boat Tim overtook them and turned the Chris-Craft to ram the Zodiac. The bow of the speedboat caught the other craft amidships, blowing out one of the side air compartments. Tim kept pushing the Chris-Craft against the sinking Zodiac until it was pressed against the Fish and Wildlife launch. As the poachers looked up at the wardens' shotguns they slumped in defeat.

Christa had never before experienced such danger or such physical excitement. With clear admiration in her eyes she turned to smile at Tim, "My God. Do you always handle things so directly?"

"They killed that deer and took something very precious from Simon," he responded with a sharp edge of hardness. With a quick mood swing he smiled at Christa, "And, you did great." Tim impulsively leaned forward and kissed her cheek.

The captain of the patrol boat called down from the bridge, "Nice job, you two. And say, isn't that Alex Greenlee's Chris-Craft."

"It certainly is, and those guys shot that deer on his island. Oh, and it's posted 'No Hunting'."

"How about coming aboard? Have a cup of coffee on the State of Washington and give us a statement."

Tim helped Christa aboard the patrol boat. When they joined the Captain he asked, "Could you relay a message to Mr. Greenlee's son that you caught those poachers? And, tell him we'll be back soon."

The Captain handed Tim the radio mike. "Tell him yourself. He's been calling every two minutes wanting to know what's going on."

As they climbed back into the Chris-Craft and Tim fired up the engine, Christa asked, "You really care a lot for Simon, don't you?"

She saw Tim grow thoughtful as if he had to carefully phrase his answer, "Yeah, I like Simon, but he's got his father's smarts, and I don't know if that's a good thing or not."

Before Christa could ask him to explain what he meant they were racing across the water at full throttle.

CHAPTER FOURTEEN

Hurricane lamps and a bright full moon reflecting off the inlet cast a warm romantic glow over the sea-facing patio. They were all enjoying an after-battle celebration and had just finished a hamburger dinner. The day's excitement had drawn Simon out of his lethargy and for once he didn't complain about Christa's cooking. When she offered him ice cream he politely responded with, "No thanks, Christa."

The adults exchanged surprised glances which Simon pretended not to notice. Then Tim remarked, "That Fish and Wildlife captain said they'd send you a letter of commendation."

"And guess what else, Simon?" asked Christa.

"What?"

"Those poachers didn't even have hunting licenses."

The boy nodded and said flatly, "Good. Dad's lawyer will want to know that when he takes 'em to court for trespassing."

Christa turned to Tim, "You'll have to testify if there's a trial."

"Can't. I'm only here for another five days. I'll give a written deposition.

You can nail them in court. And remember, you are the only witness who actually saw them carrying that deer."

"That would be a pleasure."

Simon looked imploringly at Tim, "Do you have to go away so soon?"

"I'll be back next summer." Tim raised his beer in a toast, "To our team. We did good work today."

Christa gave him a mock disapproving look as if he was being too corny. He leaned closer to her and said, "If we had some Champagne..."

"That can be arranged."

She stood and turned to Simon. "Okay, bedtime for heroes."

Before the boy could protest, Tim had him started into the house.

As they left the patio Tim asked, "Tomorrow, what's it going to be, canoeing or sailing?"

"Sailing. Just you and me."

"You got it."

Tim sat on the edge of Simon's bed listening to the boy. For once, his squeaky voice betrayed a hint of enthusiasm. "After sailing I'll e-mail mom and dad about those guys we caught and how you and Christa ran 'em down and ask them what's happening with Belle. Do you think I should tell them about old Karl?"

"Tomorrow. Your dad has enough on his mind. And, be sure and ask them if they're returning as planned. I wouldn't feel right about leaving if they're delayed."

"I hope they don't come back for a month."

Tim tousled the boy's hair affectionately and stood to leave. "Thanks, sport. See you in the morning."

When Simon was sure Tim was on his way downstairs he left the bed for his computer and logged onto the net. There was mail from The Crusher and Simon brought it up on the screen.

Hi, Cyberspace Buddy,
I can understand you not wanting me to have
your password so we can play your game.
Think on it. Do it soon, Buddy, because I'm
going on tour in a couple of days.
Your pal, Crusher.

He stared at the e-mail and began to type a response, then lifted his fingers and thought, "He's not being fair. I've got to think about this." In a state of conflict Simon shut down for the night.

Tim found Christa on the patio setting out a chilled bottle of Mums and crystal Champagne flutes. The onshore breeze had stilled. It was the evening "glass-off" when the inlet grew calm and the water took on a mirror-like sheen. The moon was now directly overhead and bright enough for him to read the bottle's label. It was a very good vintage. Christa moved close to him and said, "Adult time."

"About time."

She laughed lightly. He reached for the bottle and began to twist off the wire restraining the cork. "The Greenlees have good taste."

"A cellar full of good taste."

Tim laughed, began thumbing the cork up. "I didn't know you have a sense of humor."

"I imagine there's a lot we don't know about each other."

The cork came free with a satisfying POP! And the escaping gases propelled it over the patio wall. Tim took a whiff of the wine's bouquet and said, "Let's drink to knowing more."

He poured, filling their flutes half-way. They looked into each other's eyes and clinked glasses. Each sipped slowly, savoring the special effervescence of the bubbling wine.

Christa observed, "Only the super rich enjoy Champagne this good."

"And you're not rich?"

"Not Greenlee rich."

"Is that what you want?"

She considered his question. "It's not the money. It's the power and respect wealth brings, and calling your own shots. I suppose I should add it's the independence you get from the bullshit of others. How about you?"

He took a second sip and said, "I'd like to be rich some day. Yeah, sure. My time will come. I'm due."

She let his remark sink in and after a moment revealed her inner anxiety. "Sometimes I feel time is running out for me."

"You're young, look young."

"The way my life is going... my career and all... there's no time for anything else."

"Like a serious relationship?"

She quickly finished her wine and motioned for Tim to refill the glass. "I think I want one. I guess my biological clock is running too fast."

"Hey, you've got a man here right now. We're a family for the next few days. And, didn't I put our kid to bed?"

She liked that image and laughed softly, "But I'm not on the pill."

"I've had a vasectomy, and it's reversible."

"Really?"

"I can show you the scars, both of them."

"You are a funny man."

112

Tim topped off her flute and filled his, then reached for Christa and drew her close, "Let's take a walk."

He put a protective arm around Christa's shoulder and led her down the patio steps for the shore. Before they reached the cobble and driftwood strewn beach she stopped him and asked, "Are you on an athletic scholarship?"

"Do I look like a jock?"

"In a way, yes. And you do keep fit."

"I'm in law school, at Stanford, starting the final year. Academic scholarship. Merit and all that. I did swim on the freshman team, but Stanford doesn't pay swimmers and I have to work to stay in school. Want my full life story?"

She leaned against him. "That's enough for now. And, thank you."

They stood near a large cedar log cast up on the beach by a long ago storm. Tim remarked that the tree had been felled by loggers and had probably broken free from a log raft being towed to a sawmill. He explained that if it could be hauled off the beach and shipped to a mill the sawed timber from that single log would be worth several thousand dollars. "They float low in the water. They're called 'dead heads'. In a small boat, if you hit one head on, you're dead."

Christa didn't comment. Outdoors at night on this isolated island she usually felt uncomfortable. Then she became aware that he was holding her hand. Next to this man who had entered her life and aroused feelings she seldom experienced she felt secure. They finished their Champagne and Tim set the glasses on the log. For a long moment they looked at each other as the moonlight on the water worked its magic.

Then Tim made the first move and drew Christa into his arms. Before their lips touched, he ran his fingers tenderly, lovingly along

Christa's cheeks. There was no sunscreen on her face tonight. She felt a shiver of excitement wrack her body. With great tenderness she moved her head to kiss his palm. "We'll have only five days."

"You can live a lifetime in five days."

They drew closer and kissed with an urgency that further aroused her passion. Christa felt herself trembling with excitement. Taking the lead, she said, "Your place or mine?"

"Not the boathouse. It's damp and cold there."

As they turned from the inlet, Tim grabbed the wine bottle and glasses. They hurried hand-in-hand up the flagstone steps. Simon pulled his bedroom window curtain back an inch and looked down at the lovers passing below. He neither smiled nor frowned.

Inside, not wanting to wake Simon, they slowed to a walk and hesitated by the display cases of north coast Indian artifacts. Moonlight shining through the wide expanse of glass facing the inlet illuminated a finely carved Nootka grizzly bear ceremonial mask. Embedded in its open cedar jaws were real bear fangs. The spirit of the big coastal brown grizzly that the carving depicted held them for a moment. The power and ferocity of the ancient deity seemed to flow outward and through the glass to surround them. Instead of feeling ill-at-ease, Christa drew a primitive energy from the carving and wanted all the more to join with this man at her side.

She led him away from the display and up the stairs. Moving silently they passed Simon's door and continued on to her room. She pulled him inside and locked the door. He nodded approvingly and they moved to the open window that faced the inlet. He drew back the curtain and began to undress her. He whispered, "I want to see you, all of you, bathed in moonlight."

He slowly peeled off her sweater, and then her shirt. She was bare-breasted and her figure was fuller, more sensuous than he had expected. The moonlight's soft silver glow tinted her body enchantingly, "My God, you're beautiful."

"Surprised?"

In answer he took off his sweatshirt and gently pulled her against him, feeling her breasts flatten against his chest. She murmured sounds of pleasure and lifted her lips to his. As they kissed her fingers unfastened his belt and jeans. Their clothes fell away and each began exploring the other's body with teasingly soft touches that brought sensations of delight.

Without realizing what her body was doing, she began to writhe her hips against him in a slow, thrusting motion. Never had she felt this sexually free. When his hands cupped her breasts she whispered, "Tim, I feel actually wanton. Like some animal in heat wanting to mate. So much happened today that I never ever expected to happen..."

He silenced the panting woman with a deep, passionate kiss. Then with graceful ease he carried her to the wide bed and laid her down on the spread. She reached out for him. Propped on an elbow he smiled lovingly and ran his fingertips over her body. Liking his touch she moaned and said, "It's been a while for me..."

"Same here, and we're in no hurry are we?"

"I am..."

He held back, kissing and stroking her body until it was impossible to prolong his desire a moment longer. Even then, he controlled his thrusts until he sensed she was at a peak of responsiveness. He judged his timing by the sound of her excited panting. When he was sure she would orgasm, he allowed his own.

In the long dark hallway Simon put his ear to Christa's door. He listened to the muted sounds of their love making, but wasn't sure what he was hearing. When silence returned he retreated for his room.

Christa snuggled closer to Tim. With her passion spent she felt more relaxed. She brushed her lips across his and said simply, "Thank you."

He smiled and asked, "If we could be anywhere in the world together, where would you like to be?"

She thought a moment. "I'm happy right here with you."

"In the castle of the cyberbaron."

"Nice castle, though. Alex has good taste."

"But, what does he really love?" asked Tim.

"Alex? His business, Jennifer and Simon, and I suppose this island. He's truly brilliant, but emotionally repressed. He's a hard man to know."

"And you've worked for him how long?"

"Too long, but patience has its rewards."

He took one of her fingers between his teeth and bit it ever so gently. "And the payoff?"

"Big. What he's designed — actually what we've designed — may damn well change the world."

"But he'll take the credit. Isn't that how it works in big business?"

She lowered herself to lie across his chest and her inner fears surfaced. With a slight note of resentment she said, "I've given that man my best and received little in return. Now he's in Holland making a deal of the century that I should be part of."

"That could change the world. For the better I hope."

She brightened at that thought. "What if — not what if — because it will soon happen — everyone in the world will be able to communicate with each other like we were all connected together under the same cyberspace umbrella?"

Tim remembered Simon saying something similar but kept it to himself and asked, "In any language?"

"That's the wonder of it. No more language barriers. We've created a global operating system that's mind and eye directed."

He let her profound statement sink in and asked, "Without a keyboard or mouse?"

Her pent up enthusiasm spilled out, "An operating system that can read the mind and translate perfectly... even factoring in emotions... and every government... and the user's eyes execute commands. It's truly revolutionary."

He sat up and looked directly at Christa, "I see what you mean by big. Is it up and running?"

"The design work is always ongoing, but the prototype has been operating successfully for several months. And..."

Christa paused realizing she had said too much. Tim sensed her reluctance and offered, "And I don't have a need to know."

He ended the conversation by running a finger across her lips. She playfully bit his hand and said, "Tim, thanks for understanding."

CHAPTER FIFTEEN

Early the next morning on the sea view patio Tim patiently explained, "Simon, if you really want to be a sailor you've got to learn to tie a bowline. Now, try it again."

"Do I have to?" the boy complained as he scowled at the short length of thin rope that Tim had given him.

"It's critically important."

Simon had mastered a clove hitch and the anchor bend, but the bowline defeated his small fingers. Tim took the line, formed the primary loop and again demonstrated passing the end through the loop, under the standing line and back down into the loop. He pulled the knot taunt and said, "The beauty of a bowline is that it will never slip, yet it's easy to untie, no matter how much load it takes. Okay, sport. Once more."

He struggled, couldn't get it and complained, "Learning text typing was easier."

Christa's cheery voice came from behind them, "Good morning, guys."

They turned to see her carrying a large tray laden with breakfast. Tim stood to take Christa's heavy load, placed it on the patio table, and kissed her on the cheek. Simon noted their warm greeting and thought, "I'm sure now. They did it last night."

She proudly gestured to the tray, "Gourmet organic coffee and this morning's New York Times on my iPad. Oh, and I baked the biscuits."

"Yeah, frozen ones, cooked in the microwave," the boy said disdainfully.

Tim ignored Simon's rudeness and poured a cup of coffee for Christa. "Such service. Thank you."

She sat down beside Simon. "A bowline's a hard knot to learn. Once you get it, you'll remember how to tie it for the rest of your life. Like riding a bicycle."

"Except we don't have a bike here. And besides, there's no place to ride one."

"But there's a canoe and a sailboat…"

Simon didn't want to hear her attempt at being nice and challenged, "Bet you can't tie one."

"Bet you a smile I can, behind my back with my eyes shut."

"Prove it."

Christa took the line from Simon and put it behind her back. With a wink at Tim she closed her eyes. A moment later she handed the boy a perfectly tied bowline. For once, Simon was impressed. "Where did you learn to do that?"

"Girl Scouts."

"You, a Girl Scout," exclaimed Tim with surprise.

"Part of my secret past. How about you, Tim? Any past life secrets?"

She saw a brief look of concern flick across his face before his smile returned.

"Me. Oh, just the usual guy growing up stuff. Nothing as infamous as being a Girl Scout."

He stood and finished his coffee. Grabbing a biscuit he said, "I'm going to put the canoe in the water and check it for leaks."

"Need some help?" she asked still wondering why he was sensitive about his past.

"Thanks, but its light enough to lift alone. If it doesn't leak, we'll go canoeing later."

He reached out to affectionately touch Christa, "Maybe a Girl Scout can teach Simon to tie a bowline."

Christa began helping Simon with the knot. Holding his fingers she taught him the moves and after three attempts he tied a bowline. She congratulated him warmly. The boy only nodded as if he was thinking about something else.

She sensed his need, "What's on your mind, Simon?"

"Tim knows you're Dad's partner. Did you tell him that?"

"No. Why would I? Maybe your father did."

Simon thought on that then went off on another track, "Christa, you know all about Greenlee security. Is Dad's computer really safe from hackers?"

"There's not a computer built that's truly safe. But Alex is really clever. If someone gets close, the whole hard drive wipes out."

"'That's what I thought. Suppose someone hacked into mine, could they get into dads?"

"You're connected to his, aren't you?"

Simon nodded thoughtfully.

"Is someone trying to hack you or get your password?"

"I'm getting that feeling. Maybe I should shut down for a few days."

She summed it up, "There's your answer, Simon."

Christa watched Tim walk out of the boathouse carrying a life jacket and wearing competitive swimmer abbreviated racing trunks. With practiced ease he lifted the canoe off its saw horses and slid it into the water.

He tossed the life jacket aboard and shoved the canoe away from the dock. As it floated off he sprang into the chill inlet. His graceful dive carried him underwater and he stayed below so long that Christa grew concerned and then became truly worried.

As she stood thinking about running to the dock, Tim surfaced and swam gracefully after the canoe. With hardly any effort he muscled into the tippy craft and put on the life jacket. With a wave at Christa and Simon, he rapidly paddled off.

"He certainly looks like a college swimmer," she remarked, "Did he work out a lot at camp?"

Simon didn't comment for a moment. Then looking at her directly he said flatly, "Yeah, all the time. And you guys are lovers now, aren't you?"

In the same direct way she said, "For the next few days we are. Can you handle that?"

Without displaying any emotion, the boy nodded, stood and walked off to the house

@.

When Tim entered Simon's room the tiny Crusher character was trapped in a vast dungeon facing a huge fire-breathing two-headed monster with human arms that clutched a glittering broad sword. The boy

122

was making loud whooshing sounds that Tim guessed were simulating the roar of flames coming from the monster's spike-fanged jaws. As Crusher launched himself and sailed through the air to body slam the dragon, Tim broke the boy's concentration. "Think Crusher will get out of that alive?"

"In my game, he always wins."

Tim moved to sit beside Simon, "Sometimes in real life people lose and it makes them unhappy. Does it make you unhappy that Christa and I are, ah, close?"

"You can say you're screwing her. And if you're happy about it, then it's okay with me."

"I'm happy about it. So, we've got that understood."

Simon gave him a non-committal glance and turned to concentrate on the game. Tim moved to block his view of the screen and said with unusual force that was actually a command, "Check your mail box and then we're going canoeing."

Simon sensed his firmness and left the game to go on line. The computer's speakers announced, "Simon, you have mail."

On the screen came The Crusher's e-mail. For once, Simon showed no enthusiasm for the wrestler's message.

Hi, Simon.
Have you thought about my offer to play on line? So you'll know I trust you, I'll give you my password first. You can network with my computer using CRUSHMAN. And don't miss my match with Killer Kane next week.
Your Cyberbuddy, Crusher.

Simon filed the wrestler's e-mail. With a look of concern he turned to face Tim, "I really want to play with him. And I bet I could beat him. What do I do, Tim?"

"Is there anything in your computer you really don't want him to know about?"

"I don't have any secrets, but Dad does."

Tim thought about that and commented, "Didn't you tell me that he has his computer, ah, fire wired?"

"It's fire walled. Like a fortress. But that's not the point, Tim. I've got to get Crusher off my back." Simon shifted his fingers to the mouse, clicked on 'reply' and began typing;

Crusher.
You can not have my password.
It was wrong for you to ask for it.
Goodbye and do not e-mail me again.
Simon

Tim watched Simon's words appear on the screen. With a shrug he said softly, "It's your life, kid."

After sending the e-mail Simon turned to look for Tim and saw him walking out the door. Left alone Simon wondered what was bothering him.

CHAPTER SIXTEEN

With the moon still full, Tim and Christa sat side by side on a patio lounge warmed by the dancing flames that blazed in the round brick fireplace. The fire's warmth held off the chill from the sea bringing the couple closer together. Tonight's music was Irish. Van Morrison backed up by The Chieftains sang romantic ballads of lost battles and loves. Tim reached for the Champagne and re-filled her glass. She was feeling the wine and touched his face. "It's really lovely here, especially being with you."

"If only all this were ours."

"Don't be envious. Just accept that we're together, and this moment is ours. Soon enough, I have to go back to work."

"Developing what you were telling me about last night?"

Before she could answer, Tim leaned closer to her and asked, "Is it really happening?"

"I kid you not. It's for real."

"When the payoff comes, you could have your own island... in the

Caribbean where nights are always warm."

She laid her head against his shoulder. "Sounds romantic. And, I'd also like a penthouse overlooking Seattle, with my own private elevator, and a parking slot for a new BMW. Is that too much to ask?"

"Go for the moon. Have an island, the penthouse, and a sailboat."

She frowned and then giggled, "You know I'm not a water person."

"Really rich people have huge yachts with a captain and crew. Let me take you sailing tomorrow. You might like it. Then, when you become Christa Cyberprincess, you can dock your yacht at your own island."

His reference to cyberspace brought a frown and she said, "If Alex doesn't screw me out of what I'm due."

He brought the champagne flute to his lips, sipped, then casually asked, "As a lawyer to be, allow me to ask if you're protected by a contract?"

"When I went to work for Alex I was younger and a lot dumber. I worked my ass off, we made a lot of progress, and his dream became mine."

"And it's turning into a nightmare."

She drained her glass, sat up straight and looked into his eyes, "Tim, think of owning a big percentage of what will surely become the world's number one information technology."

"That's a bit hard to believe, Christa. I mean..."

"It does work, and it's fantastic. Believe me!"

He let that sink in for a moment and added, "From what you've been saying, just selling the design could be worth millions."

"With royalties and profit participation coming in over a lifetime, think billions."

Tim glanced at the house, "Only a locked door away..."

126

They looked at each other. Neither acknowledged the enormity of what Tim was indirectly suggesting. When she didn't comment, Tim stood and reached out for her, "This is getting too heavy for me. Let's go to bed."

She raised her glass, "I'll drink to that."

He helped Christa from the lounge chair. Holding hands they walked past the fire to the house. A burning log snapped at its center and crashed into the flames sending a small eruption of crackling sparks into the night sky.

@

On the dock, Tim and Simon were rigging the sloop. The boy noted that his buddy was being especially careful and checked the tautness of the standing rigging twice. He greased the tiller fittings and made sure the transom drain plug was screwed in tightly. When all was ready, Tim moved to the end of the dock to study the sky and water. A fresh breeze had started and Simon figured there was just enough wind for a satisfying sail.

"You expecting a blow or something?" asked Simon.

"I'm taking Christa out first, and you know how she is about the water."

"So, how was it last night?"

"None of your business, smart ass."

Simon giggled faintly, liking Tim's man-to-man gruffness. He glanced down the dock and saw her. "Here comes your girlfriend. And I bet she's got a whole tube of sun screen on her face."

"Don't tease her. She's feeling nervous enough about this already."

"Not a word."

Christa was wearing a swimsuit covered with an over-size sweatshirt and beach sandals that slap-slapped on the dock. A tennis visor shielded her nose and cheeks from the sun. She waved at them and they both sensed she was putting on a brave smile. Simon snickered, "Have fun, Tim."

"Hey, we're not going far, but if you need me I put the hand held radio aboard. Hang around the dock. We won't be long. Then the two of us can head out."

"Okay."

Christa stopped next to the sloop. Feeling apprehensive, she asked, "It's getting a bit windy, isn't it?"

"Just right for a fun sail," offered Simon. "You'll be safe with Tim."

Tim moved to help her step from the dock and into the sloop's cockpit. "Let's go before the wind kicks up."

"If it gets rough, we'll turn back, right?"

Tim whispered, "Would I chance a seasick lover?"

Without giving Christa a moment to back out, Tim freed the dock lines, jumped aboard, and raised the sail. Simon helped by pushing the hull away from the landing. They were off and the boy waved good-bye. Concentrating on getting the sloop underway, Tim didn't notice Simon standing alone and forlorn on the dock.

Feeling rejected, Simon turned to the storage locker where the fixed VHF marine radio was mounted. He opened the door and flicked on the power switch to make sure the radio was working. Then he noticed that the sloop's life jackets were still hanging in the locker. He frowned. How could Tim forget them when he was being so careful? Simon triggered the mike's transmit button. "Hey, Tim. You're some sailor. You forgot the life jackets. Over."

When no response came from the sloop, he hung up the microphone and stared at the departing boat. Tim was holding the tiller, guiding the boat for the open water of the strait, with Christa snuggled next to him.

Simon felt betrayed. Tim was supposed to be there for him, not outthere with Christa. He thought about going to his room and turning on the computer. He was close to finishing his wrestler superhero game. Then his eyes shifted beyond the inlet to the broad strait between the islands. He saw that the wind was blowing harder and beginning to start white caps. "Yeah, they'll have an exciting sail. Maybe I should hang here and wait for them."

One arm around Christa, Tim sailed confidently away from Greenlee's Island. They were still in the lee of the headland where the water was sheltered and calm. He felt her relax and said, "Not so scary, is it?"

"With you I'm feeling brave."

He pointed the boat a bit further into the wind and the hull heeled sufficiently that water splashed over the rail. Christa stiffened and said, "Don't you think it's time to put on life jackets?"

"Right. You'll have to get them. They're in the bow locker, and hang on."

Christa worked her way to the bow. Moving cautiously, she reached the little storage compartment and opened the hatch. Inside there was only an anchor attached to a length of chain and line. Holding the railing tightly she returned to Tim, "They're not there."

"Ah, shit. I left them ashore. Not to worry. We're doing fine. Besides, she's a wooden boat and can't sink."

"Please, no talk about sinking. I can't swim. Never could, and I don't want to learn out here today."

The heeling rail suddenly caught a wind wave and spray showered them. Christa fearfully clutched at Tim, "Are we alright?"

"It's okay. This is nothing. We'll make a run for the lee side of the headland. It's calmer over there. You'll see."

The water was much smoother behind the promontory and the breeze was just strong enough to move the sloop along comfortably. Christa relaxed and pulled off her sweatshirt, "This is more like it."

Nearing the rocky point, Tim slid from the helmsman's position. "Take the tiller. She's all yours."

"Oh my God. I couldn't."

He released the tiller and the boat began to turn for the headland. "You'd better, or we're on the rocks in about thirty seconds."

With another, "Oh my God," she grabbed the tiller and instinctively turned the sloop for open water. Tim gave the sheet winch handle a crank so the sail would catch the wind properly and they were again sailing smoothly. He put an arm around her shoulder and said, "You're a natural."

After a few minutes at the helm, Christa began to sense the relation between the rudder and the way the sloop pointed. With growing confidence she said, "I could learn to like sailing."

"When you have that big yacht you'll have a captain and crew to sail her."

"And a steward. I only microwave."

He laughed and moved close to her so their hips touched. For a long moment neither spoke. Then his grin faded and Tim asked, "Have you thought any more about what we talked about last night?"

She took a deep breath and looked troubled, "Let's drop that, Tim."

"I'll say no more."

The sloop left the protection of the headland and began taking water over the bow. Christa reached for Tim. Smiling again, he said, "Here comes the fun part. I'll take over now."

Where the wind blowing into the inlet was strongest Tim put the sloop on a downwind reach. With the breeze dead astern, and the full sail out at a right angle to the hull, the boat raced smoothly ahead. He again surrendered the tiller to Christa. She took command and after a few minutes of enjoying the comfortable speed said, "We're really flying."

"Downwind's always fun, but with the way it's gusting, we'd better head back."

"Just when I was enjoying it."

"Then you sail her to the dock, it's a straight shot all the way."

On the dock, Simon watched the sloop heading home and thought, "Good. Tim's not taking any chances."

Through the glare he saw Tim stand and wave. Simon put a hand over his eyes to shield them from the bright light bouncing off the water. By squinting his eyes he could see that Tim was holding the portable VHF radio. Simon moved to turn on the base station transmitter and Tim's voice came in loud and clear. "Hey, Simon. We're coming in. It's blowing kind of hard, so be ready with the dock lines."

"Got it, Tim."

Still standing, Tim studied the wind and calculated the best approach to the dock. His eyes flicked between water and sky, Christa at the tiller, and the dock they were rapidly approaching. A quarter of a mile from shore he said, "When we near the dock, I'd like you to bring the boat about for practice. Then I'll take the helm. So, do exactly what I tell you."

"Tim, maybe you should..."

"To come about heading downwind, you have to put the tiller over hard to port, that's left." Then his voice hardened, "When I say 'now' really give it your all."

They raced on and a hundred yards from the dock he called out forcefully, "Now. All the way!"

She jammed the tiller hard to port. The boat crossed the blustery wind and jibed, sending the heavy wooden boom slashing across the cockpit. Tim fought to pull in the mainsheet and screamed, "Christa, duck!"

She was paralyzed by the sudden, confusing change from serenely sailing downwind to all hell breaking loose. Then the oncoming flailing sail and boom filled her vision. Before Christa could move or make a sound the heavy boom struck her directly on the forehead. The violent impact of hard wood against brittle bone shattered Christa's skull and sent her tumbling backwards over the rail.

Simon saw it all in a blur of reflected light dazzling off the water and into his eyes. The sight and sound of the boom blasting into Christa's face and her body being flung overboard left him numb. He watched Tim stand and stare into the water, as if searching for her. A long moment passed before he kicked off his shoes, dove in, and began swimming away from the sloop. Simon realized he should do something, but shocked as he was by the sudden catastrophe, the boy could only stare.

Low in the water, Tim looked wildly about for Christa. He saw a flash of her head and hair a few yards off and sprinted on. Just before he reached her she began to sink. He made a desperate grab, but she was already underwater and going down rapidly. He gulped in a breath and dove.

In the murky freezing water, with his eyes stinging from the salt, he saw her dim form drifting downward. He stroked and kicked after her. He was deep now and his ears throbbed painfully from the increasing pressure. He shot his hand out, seized her hair, and began struggling upward. His want of air was so great that he began to see little bright bursts of light. More and more the flickering stars captured his attention. He tried to reach out for the brilliant pin points of glittering light, but his arm wouldn't move. He looked down to learn why and saw his hand clutching her hair.

Tim was shocked back to consciousness. He knew he would soon pass out from anoxia. He bit his tongue to fight it off and struggled upward. Then the dimness abruptly changed to sunlight and he surfaced with Christa in tow. He sucked in air and brought her head out of the water. Her shattered forehead made Tim gasp. Was she was still alive?

Then he looked for the sloop and with despair saw the boat blown by the breeze rapidly drifting out of reach. Despite his fatigue, he began towing the limp woman after the sailboat. He was panting rapidly, and when his want of air became too great, he was forced to stop. Only then did Tim realize Simon was standing on the dock watching them. Kicking upward as high as he could he yelled, "Simon, the canoe!"

The small, immobile figure on the dock stood shielding his eyes from the glare. When Tim's call came again, "Launch the canoe!" The boy shook off his paralysis and dashed down the dock to where it was sitting on saw horses. Then he realized the paddle was in the locker and turned about to race for it. With the paddle in hand he sprinted to the canoe. Using all his strength, Simon rolled it off the stand and tossed the paddle in. In desperate haste he slid the canoe into the water and scrambled aboard.

Utterly spent, Tim fought to keep Christa's head out of the water. He couldn't get enough air. The combined weight of their sodden clothes was pulling them down. He clawed to stay afloat, but was drawn under. Then Christa slipped from his grasp and began to rapidly sink. He made a feeble effort to dive after her, but only had the wind to descend a few feet. He looked into the dimness and watched her sink until she was nothing but a faint descending blur.

He surfaced, sucked in air, and heard Simon's frantic call, "Tim, I'm coming! Hold on!"

Then the canoe was within reach and Tim grabbed the gunwale. He was so exhausted he could barely hang on. Nothing mattered at that moment but drawing in lung full after lung full of air.

Simon looked down at his friend and dreaded what he had to ask. "Where's Christa?"

Tim didn't answer until his panting slowed. Then Simon watched him lift his head. His face and bloodshot eyes flared with anger. Between breaths he raged, "She drowned because you stood there on the dock with your thumb up your ass. What the hell took you so long to the launch the canoe?"

The boy's eyes went wide at Tim's cruel accusation. He began to stammer out his innocence, but Tim cut him off. "Nothing you can say will bring her back, so just shut the fuck up."

With the greatest difficulty, Tim struggled into the canoe. He took the paddle from Simon and started after the drifting sailboat. When he caught up with the sloop he climbed wearily aboard and put her on a heading for the dock.

Left alone in the canoe, Simon could only hold onto the paddle. As he drifted with the wind, the boy tried to understand Tim's sudden merciless attack and thought, "Maybe he really loved her."

He wanted Belle back so he could talk it all out with her. Why did they take her away? With an overpowering surge of sadness Simon turned the canoe for the dock.

CHAPTER SEVENTEEN

Simon stood behind Tim listening to him talking to the police on the base station transmitter. Tim had taken a hot shower and was wearing dry sweats, but he still shivered from the long cold immersion.

"Okay, in an hour. We'll be on the dock waiting for you."

"That's a roger. And, you might keep an eye out for the body, just in case. KMA Eight-Five-Three out."

He hung up the mike and turned to Simon. "I'm going to make myself a cup of coffee and think about what to tell the police."

"Tell them what?"

"How you just stood on the dock. Did you hate her that much?"

Tim walked off leaving Simon alone with his remorse. The boy wanted nothing more than to right the wrong he was beginning to believe was his. "If only I'd gone to the locker before they left and put the life jackets aboard. And I could have launched the canoe sooner, but the sun was in my eyes and I really didn't know what was happening."

He felt tears coming. He wouldn't cry, not now. Simon left the dock for his computer. He had an hour. An hour was enough time to change the faces on his game characters.

@

The 36 foot black-hulled police launch, towing an outboard powered inflatable boat, slammed against the pier cracking a deck board. As a crewman leaped off to secure the dock lines, Simon counted five guys. He guessed the two in casual outdoor clothes were detectives. Three men on the stern were pulling on divers' cold water wet suits. Beside them, in racks, were several gray steel SCUBA compressed air cylinders. They would soon be underwater searching the bottom for Christa's body. Simon wondered if the crabs and dogfish had started feeding on her corpse.

Before the detectives stepped off the boat Tim put a hand on Simon's shoulder. He was friendly now, again the boy's good buddy. "I'll tell them we did everything possible to save her. And I won't mention how you screwed up."

"I did get the canoe out there and saved you."

He felt Tim's hand squeezing him. "Simon, let me do the talking and you agree with everything I say. Do you understand?"

Simon, numbed by all that had happened, nodded and they walked forward to greet the two detectives.

@

In Christa's room, the police officers asked Tim questions about the drowning as they searched through her belongings. The older gray-haired detective recorded the conversation as his partner led the interrogation.

136

The detectives were professionally direct and noncommittal. They were after the facts, and if the story the young man was telling didn't satisfy them, they would probe deeper.

Tim glanced at Christa's unmade bed. He noticed that the sheets were stained from last night's love making and went on with his description of what had occurred, "So, she put the tiller hard over and the boat jibed. It happened so fast..."

The younger detective considered his statement and asked, "You're an experienced sailor, didn't you anticipate that..."

"I warned her, but she froze. Right, Simon?"

"I heard Tim yell 'Christa, duck'. And I was a long way off on the dock."

In careful, precise detail Tim described how the boom smashed into Christa's forehead and drove her overboard. He played down his desperate battle to save her and how he almost drowned himself. He put an arm around Simon's shoulders and concluded, "If Simon hadn't launched the canoe, your divers would be searching for me as well."

The silent older detective was taking it in with the skill and perception gained from twenty-two years of listening to testimony. He had caught something subliminal from the boy, some hint that not all was as described. He looked at the kid and wondered if Simon Greenlee was trying to tell him something. His partner broke into the older man's musing.

"That should wrap it up for now. There will be an inquest in a few days. In the meantime, we'll contact the deceased's family. And you'll inform the Greenlees?"

"I'll e-mail them immediately."

The detectives started for the door. Then the older man paused and turned to Simon. "Will you be all right, son?"

Simon felt Tim's fingers digging ever so slightly into his shoulder, "Yes, Sir."

The detective turned to Tim, "If you think of anything else we should know..."

"Of course, and thanks for coming so quickly."

On the dock, Tim and Simon stood with the detectives watching the divers unload Christa's body from their inflatable boat. They had already wrapped her in a green plastic tarp. One of the divers called to the detectives, "Found her right where they said she went down."

The younger detective turned to Tim, "If you'll identify the deceased..."

Looking grim, Tim followed the young detective aboard the launch. Simon tagged along behind the men. The senior detective handed him a business card, "Son, if you'd like to give us any more information, I'm only a call away," and stepped ahead to join his partner.

No one noticed the silent boy behind them who peered at the shrouded body on the stern deck. He wondered if she could possibly still be alive.

Christa lay face up in a pool of water that was spreading across the teak deck planking. The younger detective drew back the tarp covering her face. Her battered, indented forehead and the bluish-gray sheen of her skin left no doubt that she was very dead. Looking at her corpse Tim murmured, "Yes, that's Miss Carter."

Simon moved a hand to cover his mouth and still the gasp he felt coming. The boy was surprised that the sun-screen on Christa's face had survived her death. He looked up at Tim and their eyes locked. This time, when Tim laid a hand on Simon's shoulder to guide him off the police launch, the boy flinched.

@

Tim stood behind Simon dictating an e-mail to the Greenlees. He was impressed with the boy's typing skill, but as Simon had said, soon any dummy, and in any language, could use a computer.

He phrased his last paragraph carefully, "... if there is any change in your return schedule, please let me know. Be assured that I will be here with Simon as long as necessary. Despite the tragedy, he is well, and considering what happened, in good spirits. Sincerely, Tim."

When Simon had sent the e-mail Tim moved for the door. The boy turned to stare coldly at him and after a moment asked, "Where are you going?"

"Simon, understand this. From now on, I'm in charge here, and I ask the questions. And my first order is to leave your computer on and come with me."

He grabbed Simon's hair and dragged him downstairs to the hall leading to his father's work area.

Simon had never felt such a shock of pain and violence. He wanted to scream at Tim. But he knew that if he exposed his fear Tim would hurt him again.

When they reached the steel door Tim released Simon and picked up a manila envelope that lay on the floor beneath the retina scanner and signature recognition pad. Simon moved closer and watched Tim pull a carbon copy of some sort of medical form from the envelope. Simon was surprised to see his father's signature at the bottom of the form. Tim then withdrew the stylus from its receptacle and began writing 'Alex Greenlee' on the signature recognition pad. As Tim copied Alex's name again and again his eyes shifted repeatedly between the pad and Greenlee's carbon copy signature.

When his counterfeiting efforts failed to trigger the lock he pulled a jeweler's loupe out of a pocket and carefully examined the signature sample. Simon heard him whisper, "Okay, a little more pressure on the 'G' and 'e'."

He signed again and the lock's entry light switched to green. Tim snapped his fingers and said happily, "One down, Simon."

"Nobody goes in Dad's office. He wouldn't even let you in when you helped him with the door."

Tim spun and glared at Simon who drew back fearful of being struck, "Until now, smart ass."

Simon's eyes shifted to the carbon paper. Curiosity overcame fear. He asked, "Where did you get my father's signature?"

"I stole your medical release form your dad signed when he brought you to camp. That place is so old fashioned they still use carbon paper."

"And the amount of pressure he used to sign his name shows by how much the carbon is compressed and deposited on the paper."

"You're pretty sharp, Simon."

"Bet you can't get past the retina scanner."

"Bet you a billion dollars I sure as hell can."

Tim picked up the manila envelop lying by the door. He opened the flap and Simon watched him withdraw a life size color photograph of a human eye. The image was incredibly sharp and he knew that it was his father's eye. "So, that's why you have a Nikon and took all those pictures of me and my family at camp."

"Right again, Simon."

He raised the enlargement to the eye scanner and held it steady before the cathode ray tube. The electronic beam swept over the photo and recognized what it was programmed to identify. A digital voice responded, "You may enter."

Tim reached for the door and grasped the handle. Then he paused and turned to Simon. "Have you ever been in there?"

"Sure. Sometimes I help my dad."

"And you learned his password. Right?"

Simon only stared. Tim crowded against him and looked down at the boy. His expression was hard, determined, "I'm going to need your help turning the silent alarm off."

When Simon refused to respond, Tim opened the door and looked inside. Simon tried to squeeze past him into the workroom. Before he could enter, the man's hand shot out and grasped him by the neck stopping him.

"So there is a silent alarm and it senses movement. Is that why you want inside first?"

He held the boy back and gazed about Greenlee's work area. No Doctor Frankenstein's laboratory here, but were there other invisible electronic guards lurking? What Tim saw was a surgically sterile, all putty colored, computer research facility, an electronic throne room where a cyberbaron ruled. Even the large window, with a view of the dense forest beyond the backyard, had putty colored drapes. Every metal box containing the latest computer equipment was covered with custom fitted breathable transparent plastic shrouds. Not one item in the room gave a hint of the personality of the man who had created a Fortune Five Hundred empire in this antiseptic space.

Simon looked up at Tim and saw his face glowing with awe, as if he'd wriggled into an ancient Egyptian pyramid and beheld a gold encrusted

141

mummy. "It's like he's in some kind of holy shrine," thought Simon, "I wonder if Dad placed a curse on his stuff."

Simon had viewed several Discovery Channel television specials about the opening of royal tombs and remembered a low budget re-enactment of Carter's momentous 1922 discovery of Tutankhamen's crypt. The actor's words were forever implanted in the boy's memory. In his mind he heard the soundtrack from that documentary:

"What do you see in there, Carter?" asked the archaeologist's assistant.

"Things. Wonderful things," came the enthralled voice from the Pharaoh's burial vault.

Simon's fantasy was shattered by Tim's hand grabbing his hair and shaking his head so hard he thought his teeth would fall out, "Turn off the alarm, Simon."

He looked up at the man's stern, demanding face and glared back to defy him. The pain grew worse and the boy gritted his teeth expecting more.

"Is your hearing impaired, Simon?"

"I can't reach it. The switch is over the door jamb."

Tim ran his fingers along the top of the molding and found the alarm switch. He flicked it off and in a less harsh voice said, "Very good, Simon. Let's continue our friendly cooperation."

As Simon watched, Tim cautiously stepped into the workroom and began pulling plastic covers off the computers and their ancillary equipment.

"Well make my day!" Tim exclaimed happily, "Your father left his computer on. Some of us insecure folks, like your dad, fear turning them off on the remote chance that they won't boot up again. Good of Alex. Saves me from battling through his security." On the screen Tim scanned icons and clicked on Alex's operating system file. Nothing.

He fought to keep his growing frustration from Simon, "But there's one small problem. It seems his new operating system file is password protected." Back to his 'good buddy' mode, Tim asked casually, "If you remember it let me know."

He continued moving about the room studying the various components that were connected to a central processing unit. His fingers running over the casings suggested a lover's gentle though passionate touch. A round object larger than a basketball and protected by a plastic shroud caught Tim's interest. He carefully removed the cover and muttered, "What the hell is that?"

Tim walked around a large globe of the earth. Attached to thin wire stalks projecting from the surface of the globe were twelve models of small satellites. Their placement suggested they were in orbit like GPS satellites. He flicked one with a finger and it vibrated with such intensely that a satellite flew off. Simon called angrily, "Hey, watch it. That's not a toy."

The boy's heated response suggested he'd damaged something important and Tim feigned regret, picked up the model and attached it to the wire, "Sorry, Simon. I can see its earth with satellites in orbit, but what's it represent?"

Without a change of expression Simon skillfully lied, "It's an idea of mine and I've been working on it with Dad. It's a real time worldwide radiation reporting system anyone with a computer can log on to. Since what happened in Japan at Fukushima everyone should have one."

That explanation didn't hold Tim's interest. He turned to a large printer, called an X-Y plotter that was designed to handle 36 inch wide roll paper. The plotter held his attention for almost a minute. When he finished his careful, prolonged inspection of the workroom he sat at the main terminal and explored its intricate features.

The boy watched Tim gently reach out to touch an optical eye scanner that sat over the monitor screen that projected outward on a flexible stalk at a height to match the user's eye level. Simon was reminded of the measuring device that Doctor O'Connor, the family ophthalmologist, used when he tested his eyesight

Tim peered into the optical scanner and said, "Is this how the operating system reads eye movement?"

"You figure it out."

"So, the movement of the eye to an icon on the monitor triggers a command. And, a right or left eye blink serves the same function as clicking a mouse. Not a hell of a lot faster, is it?"

He turned to Simon, hoping he had tricked the boy into revealing more. Simon's response was an angry glare.

He watched Tim reach for the brain-wave receptor head set and place the collector probes on his skull. It did look like a prop out of a science fiction movie, but it was actually something his father had modified from a medical EEG brain scanning device. Tim began to stuff the various probes between the strands of his hair so the receptors would touch his scalp. His unfamiliarity with the sensor frustrated Simon and he said, "You don't need to do that. Just put it on your head like a hat. It's so sensitive it doesn't need to touch your skull."

"What's it for?"

"It translates your thought into different languages. So far it works for French, German, and Spanish. We'll get to Chinese and Russian next."

With a pissed-off look Tim did as the boy told him. Then, back to being Simon's good buddy, he said matter-of-factly, "And your father used you as a test subject."

Simon remained silent as Tim removed the brain-wave receptor and took two minutes to familiarize himself with the computer's various ancillary features. He found a bank of phone and Internet satellite up link Off/On switches. With a knowing grin he told Simon, "Your father's a control freak. Nobody e-mails or calls from here if he cuts the up links. Pretty clever. I'll shut down the phones and broadband. Just so you don't get any ideas."

Tim rubbed his hands together as if about to give a piano recital and placed his fingertips on the keyboard. Tim hesitated and turned to give Simon a triumphant glance. With a decisive flourishing movement he leaned forward and began typing. A list of household computers networked to Alex's appeared on the monitor. Then Tim put the cursor on Simon's name and clicked. The boy's list of recent e-mails filled the screen.

"You left your computer on, Simon. Not environmentally correct, you know."

"Dad does, and you told me to leave it on."

Tim gently rapped Simon's skull with his knuckles, "Don't get cheeky with me. Take a close look at the screen."

Simon moved closer to the monitor and Tim gloated, "No secrets in this house, Simon. There's a complete list of your Internet history on your Dad's screen. Did you know that he knows about your video game purchases?"

Simon's gut tensed and he felt a deep twinge of guilt. His father must be aware that he was using the company credit card to buy video games. He defended himself by thinking, "They're just computer log-ins junk."

Tim understood Simon's troubled squirming and played on the boy's all too obvious guilt. Now to rub it in and break him down, "And then there was that Crusher poster. How do you explain that nineteen-ninety-five plus postage and handing charge?"

Simon's jaw dropped, His eyes went wide, He gasped and stammered, "You couldn't know that — couldn't know how much I paid. Because it's not on the log-in... unless..." Then Simon understood the devastating revelation of Tim's enormous betrayal.

"You set me up. You counterfeited that poster offer so I'd order it, didn't you! You're a Crusher poser! You did this so I'd give you my game password and then you could hack into Dad's secure CPU! It didn't work and I'll never give it to you!"

"And you're a very astute kid. I give you high marks for that." Tim's thoughts raced. "I've got to get that kid's e-mail account. How? Beat it out of him? Torture?" Tim realized he wouldn't learn Simon's password through coercion. He had to outsmart the kid. And now he knew how. He shouted, "Get the hell out of here Simon and let me work."

Tim watched the boy flee and then leaned back in Alex's orthopedically correct desk chair. He knew with the certainty of tomorrow's sunrise that Simon was racing upstairs for his computer, "and now I have him."

Tim reached out and with the flip of a switch restored the boy's satellite e-mail up-link.

CHAPTER EIGHTEEN

In his bedroom Simon sat before the glowing monitor. His trembling fingers rested on the computer's keyboard. He was in a major state of emotional distress and couldn't decide if he should first e-mail his parents, alert San Juan Islands Security, or contact the old detective whose card was in Simon's desk drawer.

For a moment he gave in to despair and allowed his head to sink into his hands. He took a deep breath and stood up to glance out the window. Today he noticed that the sky was clear, the inlet calm, and that it was low tide. When a raven flew by and cawed for no other reason than to make itself heard, Simon forced himself back to his dilemma.

Simon picked up his desk phone. No dial tone. He felt badly betrayed. Tim had used his attachment to the real Crusher in an attempt to steal his e-mail account password. With that never to be revealed secret Tim could intercept his e-mail and send lies to his parents. With a deep feeling of violation he thought, "Goodbye Crusher."

His attention left the keyboard and he looked outside. His eyes held on the sloop and canoe. They brought him back to his fear of Tim.

Simon returned to the computer, and it opened to the comforting glow of his e-mail page. Now that he could send out a cry for help, he might live through this day after all. Then he heard the computer's voice, "Simon, you have mail."

Three seconds later he began to read a cheery note from his mother. With a sudden dreadful shock he realized Tim had never told his parents about Crista's death.

> Dearest Simon,
> All goes well for your father, although there
> have been contract haggles which slow our
> negotiations. We will let Tim know if our
> schedule changes. We're so glad Tim is there
> to look after you.
> Please let us know how you are and what you
> have been doing...

In Alex's studio Tim read the opening lines of Jennifer's e-mail and sprinted upstairs. He burst through the door and violently knocked Simon away from the keyboard. Tim found that the boy was already composing a response to his mother's note:

> Dear Mom,
> Tim is not my friend anymore. Please come
> home. Tim killed Christa and I'm next! Please
> call Island Security and then the police. Tell
> them about Tim now!!!!

Tim quickly canceled Simon's damning note and snarled, "You

almost did me in you fat little prick!'"

'Fat little prick' hurt more than Tim's brutality. Then he realized Tim had tricked him and taken over control of his computer.

"Sorry to be so rough. Okay, kid? First we'll do some creative editing. Your mom and dad are going to really like what they'll read. Something like, ah... 'we're having fun hiking, canoeing, and sailing' and so on. Then you'll ask about Belle, so they'll know you're thinking of her. You know, to add a touch of sincerity."

After Tim sent a comforting e-mail to Jennifer and Alex he thought, "Alex will buy that. What he wants most is to sign the deal."

Simon was still shocked that Tim had not informed his parents of the drowning, "You told the police you would let my folks know that Christa was dead!"

"I lied. That would only worry them. Next we reset your password so I become you. And you become a cybernonperson. Now let's change your password." With a hint of growing madness Tim laughed and asked, "Any suggestions for the new one?"

Tim then began resetting Simon's e-mail password. His attention was so focused on the complicated instructions that Simon saw that he might escape. He dropped to his knees and out of Tim's field of vision. Not daring to look over his shoulder, Simon silently crawled across the carpeted floor and out the door. Tim decided to remain by Simon's computer and wait for the Greenlees' response to Simon's new persona. But what if they should call? They won't. They're so addicted to e-mail they wouldn't think of using a phone. He looked for Simon. The kid had vanished.

As Simon hurried down the hallway he slowed to look out a window and focused on the dock. His eyes held on the sloop and the canoe, then roved to the locker by the boathouse, "The radio! The power's on, so it's got to be working. I'll radio security, then the cops. Come on. Get going before he gets you."

Tim stood, peered out the window, and caught sight of Simon heading for the dock. As Tim started after him, the computer alerted him to an e-mail. When Tim had the Greenlee's reply on Simon's monitor he read that they would be returning as scheduled.

He reread the e-mail twice more looking for any hidden meaning or a suggestion they were trying to trick him. It was typically Greenlee polite. With rising excitement he thought, "They bought it. Okay! Something's going right today. I'll acknowledge their arrival time and reassure them once more". He began typing, "Dear Mr. and Mrs. Greenlee…"

Thinking Tim must still be in his room, Simon decided to make a run for the boathouse and use the radio to call for help. He dashed along the dock and ripped open the locker doors. As he reached to turn on the radio he moaned in defeat. The microphone was missing. With growing panic he knew he had to find somewhere to hide, but there was no hiding place Tim couldn't find. He must flee and right now.

He could take the skiff, or Dad's speedboat, or even the canoe, and escape. The canoe. "I can handle a canoe, but it's so slow, and where's the paddle?" He remembered he left the paddle and a life jacket leaning against the back of the locker when he'd brought the canoe back after Christa drowned. Simon corrected himself, "After Tim killed her, and he'll do the same to me next."

After a look down the dock Simon grabbed the paddle and a life jacket and rushed for the upside down canoe. He carefully tucked them where they wouldn't fall out. Then Simon noticed the door to the boathouse was ajar, "I bet I could run Dad's skiff or the Chris-Craft.

The water's calm. I'd be in Friday Harbor in half an hour. Oh boy!"

Simon entered the boathouse and locked the door behind him. He knew Tim had a key for the door, but locking it eased his fear. Simon quickly discovered that the gas tank that fueled the outboard had been removed from the skiff and there was no key in the Chris-Craft's ignition switch. Tim was thinking ahead of him. "When he broke into Dad's studio he didn't have the radio mike. Maybe he hid it upstairs."

In the dim apartment above the boats there was no trace of the microphone, but there sat Tim's laptop. Simon raised the screen, ran his fingers across the keyboard and glanced at the mini external hard drive. "Real hacker stuff."

Now on familiar ground he powered up Tim's computer.

Rows of folders filled half the desktop. And each was identified by initials. His eyes held on one named 'BD'. With the mouse Simon opened Tim's file on Belle Dubois. Moments later he had the latest document on the screen and read:

TO: IMMIGRATION & NATURALIZATION
        SERVICE
SUBJ: EMPLOYMENT OF ILLEGAL ALIEN
        BELLE DUBOIS
FROM: A CONCERNED CITIZEN

It has come to my attention that Alex Greenlee of Greenlee Electronics has for two years employed an undocumented illegal alien, who may be a left wing extremist and wanted by authorities in her home country of Haiti for terrorist...

Simon was truly shocked by the revelation that Tim had sent INS the poison pen e-mail. "How could he do that to Belle?"

The boy hacked on and found a file of past Crusher e-mails to himself. With a feeling of deep hurt he realized that all the messages that Crusher had sent him since he had ordered the poster had indeed come from Tim, "He learned about Crusher from Dad when he helped hang that new security door. I bet they even joked about me. It was all about using Crusher to get my password so he could e-mail my parents and read what they were sending me — and he could even pretend to be me and get into Dad's hard drive!"

Lost in the absorbing documents of Tim's treachery, Simon ran through file after file from the most recent entry about his family to the formation of Greenlee Electronics seven years ago. There were scanned newspaper photos and stories of his father's meteoric rise in the electronics world. "He's kept a scrapbook, like he was stalking us."

Then Simon discovered a file about the summer camp he had just attended and a copy of Tim's letter of application for a camp counselor's position, "And he took that job to get close to us."

He opened a file marked 'AGA' and discovered it was an animated computer game. With horrified fascination Simon watched the realistic shooter video. The faces of two characters looked familiar. The man with the gun was Tim. The other man, who died before Simon's eyes, was his father. He reached for the joystick and tried to reverse the game's outcome and bring his father back to life. Simon impulsively cried aloud, "No, Dad!" but the man lying in the rubbish strewn mean street didn't rise.

Simon broke the spell of dread and continued searching more Greenlee files. He soon realized that Tim had built an electronic personality profile of his father. He read on until a scanned newspaper

152

story grabbed his attention. He stopped scrolling and read aloud in his squeaky, high-pitched voice, "The promising start-up Silicon Valley company DataThink was recently acquired by Greenlee Electronics in a hostile takeover"

"It wasn't hostile, Simon. It was criminal."

The boy spun to find Tim looming over him. He tried to slip out of the chair and flee, but the man's hands clamped on his shoulders forcing him to sit.

"In case you need help translating the business section, that means your father ripped me off. DataThink was my company and he vaporized me."

Simon knew it was common practice for big companies to swallow up little ones and take over profitable lines of research. He shook his head in denial, but inwardly he sensed Tim's accusation might be true.

Tim raged on tight-lipped with hatred, "He stole what I worked years to create. Your father's a thief. And, right now he's in Holland, selling what he robbed from me. And you, smart ass little turd, are going to help me get back what's mine. Understood?"

Simon looked up at Tim and saw the same cruel hardness he had revealed when accusing him of allowing Christa to drown. Tim grabbed his laptop, yanked the terrified boy out of the chair and shoved him toward the door.

Outside, Tim held Simon by the back of the neck and forced him along the dock. He paused by the sloop. With a menacing wicked grin, he asked, "Shall we go sailing?"

CHAPTER NINETEEN

Tim shoved Simon into his father's workroom and pointed to the chair before the main computer. "Sit there until I tell you to do otherwise."

Simon watched him place the laptop next to his father's computer, plug in the power cord, and turn the machine on. Then Tim moved behind Simon and clamped his hands on his shoulder until he yelped.

"Let's make this easy, Simon. Now click on your father's operating system and type in his password."

"I don't know it!"

"You've sat in this chair how many times? Dozens of times, hundreds, while he tested my operating system on you. And you didn't watch him type his password. Come on, Simon."

The boy turned to look up at Tim and sincerely said, "He was always in his programs before he let me in, and that's the truth."

"What's your password then?"

"So you can use it to enter Dad's mainframe. Won't work. I've tried."

"Prove it. I dare you."

Simon suppressed a faint surge of hope that began to grow. He'd actually tricked Tim and said, "It's Belle, 'cause I really like her, and I know what you did to her and Christa, and maybe old Karl. At least Belle's alive."

With a tone of outraged injustice Tim snapped, "I had nothing to do with Mannheim's disappearance."

"Then how come you knew his last name."

"I made it my business to know everything about everyone on this island, smart ass."

"And you got rid of them one by one. And you know what, Tim? You'll never get away with it. You killed Christa. They'll hunt you down. And even if you do get away with Dad's software, nobody's going to want to deal with you."

"But who am I, Simon? Just some guy with a law degree earned under another name. You have to be smart to pass the bar the first time. And this guy and that lawyer are going to vanish. New identity. New face. Accounts waiting in offshore banks. And what do you think about that? It's Tim's Plan A. And of course there's B and C."

Tim moved so quickly. Simon feared he was going to strike him. Instead he shoved Simon aside, "I don't have time for your crap. We'll go straight in."

Tim began typing 'Bell'.... and suddenly froze. Furious now, he yelled, "You little shit. He fire walled his computer with 'Belle" in case you tried to enter. You knew that didn't you smart ass, and you set me up for a hard drive wipe out. So where does he keep a backup."

"On a memory stick on his key ring and it's in Holland smart ass."

Instead of exploding, Tim laughed and gave Simon a gentle pat on the cheek. The boy recoiled fearfully.

"Hear this, Simon. If I don't get what I want now I'll ruin him with a lawsuit later. And I spent four years in law school preparing to destroy your father — one way or the other."

"I can't give you the password because I don't know it!"

"You're a lot like your father, devious and tough, but this time, Simon, I win."

He grabbed Simon's chair and shoved it to where the boy could view the monitor screen. Then Tim sat and placed his hands on the keyboard, "We're going to play twenty questions, or maybe two thousand, but we are going to find his password. Okay, Simon let's start with the obvious. With a maniacal snarl Tim pulled his Swiss Army Knife from a pocket, smashed it against the desk top, "If you try any funny stuff I'll slice you left ear off, and I don't mean maybe."

Tim turned to his laptop and brought up a long list of short words and numbers he had gathered that Alex might use as a password. Simon read down the categories and saw the names and birthdays of the Greenlees and his mother's family going back two generations, his father's college nickname 'Greenie', the license plate numbers of his parents' BMWs kept at the corporate office garage in Seattle, and odds and ends of possible passwords that Tim had assembled from his electronic profile of the family. When Tim's list ended, he turned to Simon, "Your turn. What's your dad's favorite ice cream?"

"Coffee pecan"

He typed in coffee and then pecan. Nothing. "What's his favorite holiday?"

"Halloween."

Nothing. "Hell, I forgot to try your birthday."

They went on and on for another hour until Simon began yawning from boredom and said, "You'll never find it."

With a hard look Tim said, "Let's try a different road. Who does he hate the most?"

"You, if he knew what you were doing. And you hate him."

Tim leaned back in the chair, seeming confused. He rubbed his cramped hands together and then turned to stare at Simon. "Did he ever mention my company, DataThink?"

Simon shook his head and Tim went on with his musing, "He took something very precious from me. Your house and this island could have been mine if..."

Tim froze as if seeing a ghost and murmured, "Do I dare...", and turned back to the keyboard. Very slowly, carefully he began typing DataThink. It was crunch time for Tim. He held his breath and noticed his heart beating furiously. A moment later the computer's audio speakers announced, "Password confirmed. You may now enter."

Elated, Tim laughed manically as Alex's file directory appeared on the monitor, "As they say, Bingo!"

With a paranoid mood swing Tim spat out his bitterness, "He used me, stole what I created, and even took my company name. And your father is so full of himself he didn't even remember doing it."

Typing full speed, Tim brought up the DataThink files and found a schematic programming diagram, "That's my initial concept of the operating system. I wrote that program."

More complex diagrams appeared on the screen. Tim leaned forward studying them and observed, "Here's where he took off from my original work. Brilliant, too."

Tim pushed his chair back and turned to the boy, "Do you know what this means, Simon?"

Simon withdrew into his sullen arms folded over his chest posture, and glared at Tim.

"It means smart ass that you will not become the richest kid in the world."

He returned to the computer and began a long monologue of mumbled curses that ended with him bellowing, "This is outrageous!"

Facing Simon, he demanded, "Do you have any idea what your father has done with my work?"

"Yeah, he made it into something important."

"He has created a monster, a one man disaster for the world. Or was it your idea little fat boy."

Simon was hurt by the truth of Tim's insult and stammered, "I don't understand"

Tim reached for his Swiss Army knife, opened a blade and pointed it at Simon, "What he's done is create a system to link everyone's computer to a single world-wide gargantuan mainframe. As you said, and Christa said, and I thought it was just bullshit, he's going to get everyone linked to a single program under a world-encompassing cyberspace umbrella."

He pointed to the globe and its quavering model satellites, "And that, you little prick, is how Greenlee and his European partner will entice governments to pay billions for the rights. His bit of corrupt genius will destroy what little freedom we have left. It's truly evil, Simon. And you helped him create it."

With an abrupt mood swing Tim added, "And it's pretty damn brilliant. As some say, if you can't beat 'em, join 'em."

He lunged at the boy and knocked him off the chair, "Too bad for you, Simon. Now get your ass over to the X-Y printer and load in a new roll of paper. This diagram's going to run twenty-thirty pages."

"You could download it into your computer."

"Because I don't trust you or your father, I want a hard copy. Get going."

Simon retreated from Tim's increasingly chaotic behavior and moved across the workroom for the X-Y plotter/printer. He reached for a fresh roll of paper and chanced a glance at Tim. He was fully absorbed at the computer studying the programming diagrams that he scrolled one-by-one on the screen.

At that instant the fearful boy felt certain that once Tim had what he wanted, the crazed man would take revenge by killing him. His eyes searched the room seeking some way to escape. The door held his focus. Over the upper jamb he could just see the switch that would activate the silent alarm. If he could turn it on, the motion sensor would be energized and an automatic alert transmitted via its dedicated microwave link to San Juan Islands Security at Friday Harbor.

Simon began unwrapping a fresh roll of printer paper. He would need a stick, or something to extend his reach in order to trigger the silent alarm switch. He placed the new fifty-foot roll of paper on a table and opened the printer to take out the old one. It was almost empty. When he had extracted the thin three foot long heavy cardboard roller Simon realized he was holding a tool that might be long enough to reach the switch. Another glance at Tim told the boy he was still totally focused on the computer monitor.

Holding the stiff cardboard tube he approached Tim and said, "I think I got it in right."

Muttering annoyance, Tim stood and crossed the room to check the boy's installation. As he turned his back to Simon the boy asked pleadingly, "I have to uh pee?"

Intent on checking the printer, Tim waved permission for Simon to leave the room and said, "Be back here in two minutes or I'm coming after you."

Clutching the empty paper roller, Simon hesitated by his father's computer and switched the satellite phone link to ON. As he reached for the knob he glanced at Tim. He was fully absorbed running a print test and watching the results roll out of the machine. Simon went up on his tiptoes and extended the roller as far as he could reach. The end of the tube rubbed along the upper door molding and Simon felt the cardboard scrape over the switch. He couldn't tell if he had activated the silent alarm or not and didn't dare to make a second attempt. Without looking at Tim, he fled the workroom.

CHAPTER TWENTY

Sixteen miles away on the east side of the Friday Harbor marina, by the Union 76 gas dock, sat the squat, newly built, concrete block office of San Juan Islands Security. Over the past two decades the trendy town had boomed. Home protection services had prospered as developers made fortunes from the newly arrived rich who wanted their mini-estates guarded against imagined threats. Business was good and the work was easy for San Juan Island Security

Inside the office, linked to clients by the latest electronic security systems, the day shift patrolman was pouring a cup of coffee and thinking about taking the ferry to Seattle to attend the Sea Hawks football game. A wealthy client had given him a pair of box seat tickets on the fifty yard line in appreciation for chasing off a scruffy boater who had tied up to his private mooring. There was this hot girl he'd met at the Pikes Place Market who was a Sea Hawks fan. While he was buying a Sarah Clementson original watercolor calendar at Watercolors Fresh Daily, she brought three for her family back east, and they got to talking...

His daydream was shattered by the angry buzz of an alarm. He glanced at a blinking red light on the master control panel and swore, "Ah, hell. It's the Greenlee's."

He called to his older partner, the day supervisor, who was working outside polishing their patrol boat's chrome fittings. "Ernie, the Greenlees' silent alarm just went off."

Ernie capped the can of Meguiar's and hurried into the office. He looked at the client status board and said, "They're away, you know."

"But they got people staying there. Could be a false alarm. How about calling?"

"You know Mister Greenlee's orders. If the alarm goes off, we go flat out and armed. And you heard about that drowning at Greenlee's'"

"It's sixteen miles and I got a ferry to catch."

"If it is a false alarm, we'll be back in an hour. Grab the shotguns and let's haul ass."

Ninety seconds later Island Security's 26-foot Boston Whaler roared out of Friday Harbor. By the time the boat reached open water its twin 300 horsepower engines were driving the Whaler at thirty-five knots. Ernie figured if the water stayed calm they'd be at the Greenlee's dock in just under a half an hour. "Most likely it's a false alarm, but then again..."

@

By the time Simon reached Christa's room the patrol boat was underway. Though the boy wasn't sure if the alarm had worked or not he knew Tim had turned on the satellite up link and he could e-mail using Christa's laptop.

He sat down at Christa's computer. The Ethernet jack was still plugged into the modem. Then he realized he didn't know her password, and gave a muted cry of anguish, "Okay, don't be a wimp. Go to your room and use your own computer. But he'll find me by then and I'm toast. The Phone!" He grabbed the phone and heard a dial tone. "Call Island Security first. They'll get here faster than the cops. And then the old detective, what was his name? And the phone numbers? Oh shit! His card's in my desk. Okay. Don't panic. Think."

Simon's father had made him memorize Island Security's phone number, and the boy carefully punched the numbers. He heard the ring followed by a recorded message, "You have reached Island Security. Your call is important to us and will be answered within one minute. Please hold on. We'll always be here for you."

"One minute! I could be dead in one minute."

Tim left the printer, satisfied it would perform correctly, and sat at Alex's computer. He typed in the print command and thought, "I'll be doing this with my eyes before long."

Now all that he had planned, had dreamed and agonized over, would soon come to pass. He allowed himself a moment to relax and stretched to ease the growing tension in his back. He took half a dozen deep from the belly slow breaths to calm his mind. Tim closed his eyes and imagined the shock Alex Greenlee would feel when he read his good-bye message on the cyberbaron's computer. He glanced at the large roll paper printer. The diagrams were coming off the roller nicely and he noticed that the colors were bright and the programming symbols distinct.

As he rocked back in the chair his eyes caught sight of the satellite phone switch, "Shit, the kid turned it on." He realized that in his moment of

165

inattention, when his back was to Simon, the boy had restored the satellite up link. "The kid could have called the police or Island Security by now. Could have! He's so sharp he's already done it."

As he rose from the chair Tim switched the phone off. With cold calculating clarity he thought, "He's killing me!" Tim burst out the door at a run bellowing, "Simon!"

Tim's distant shout shocked Simon out of his dread and he knew he'd been found out. He sat frozen and stared with disbelief at the dead phone. Then the instinct to survive that is inherent in the human spirit kicked in. Simon forced himself out of the chair and fled.

The boy knew the house well, better than his parents, better than Belle or the expensive, socially prominent architect who had designed the Greenlee's splendor palace. Fortunately for Simon, the architect had drawn doors where no door ought to be and storage areas with small windows that became escape hatches to decks that led to other rooms,

Simon took advantage of his home habitat and, with his heart pounding in fear, he eluded Tim. As Simon fled, he formulated a plan of escape that depended on reaching ground level without getting caught.

San Juan Security's phone relay transferred Simon's call to the patrol boat. Ernie picked up the shore to ship receiver and checked the status of the call. It had originated from the Greenlees. But there was no one on the line. His young partner, thinking about the Sea Hawks game, said hopefully, "They could have been reporting a false alarm."

"Forget football, will you."

Tim's footsteps pounded closer and Simon darted into a huge upstairs linen closet. Using the shelves as a ladder, he climbed to the top shelf and silently slid the door shut. Pushing aside a stack of giant bath towels he wriggled behind them. By pulling the towels back he was able to fully conceal himself. He had hid there before when playing hide and seek with Belle. She had never found his secret place. He lay panting, fighting to control his rapid breathing. He was sure that if he didn't Tim would find him.

Throwing over beds, peering into showers and walk-in closets, Tim charged through the second story hunting the boy. Simon could hear his angry swearing and knew Tim was growing more manic by the minute. When he reached the linen cabinet and slid aside the wide door he paused to bring himself under control.

He imagined himself in Simon's position and tried to figure out where the boy might have gone. He began to reason out loud, "If he did reach the cops, which I doubt, then he's holed up somewhere waiting for them. If he'd didn't, he's trying to figure out a way off the island. He can't use the powerboats, so it's either the canoe or the sloop. Then I'd better..."

Behind the towels Simon heard Tim's every word and held his breath. He knew that the slightest sound or movement would mean his death. He began to feel light-headed from lack of oxygen and sucked in a tiny stream of air though his nostrils. What came into his nose were minute particles of cotton dust and he fought to hold back a sneeze. As his body began to convulse, the closet door slammed shut. He heard Tim walking away and pressed his face deep into a towel to smother the sound of his sneeze. He thought it was loud enough to wake the world, but to Simon's relief Tim's footsteps retreated down the hall and faded away.

He knew that Tim was on his way to the dock. "He'll find the paddle I put in the canoe. If he does, I'll never get off the island. How do I stop him?"

His mind raced in a jumble of ways to distract Tim long enough for him to reach the dock and launch the canoe. He started down the hall and passed his room. He glanced inside and on impulse grabbed his bow and quiver of target arrows. His orange foul weather jacket was hanging on a bedpost and he pulled it on. Peering down the wide staircase he looked for Tim and thought, "Boy, do I need the real Crusher now."

Suddenly, like divine intervention, he conceived a plan to divert Tim. Reaching the ground floor he moved cautiously for the entertainment center and let himself inside. His often viewed DVD of "Crusher's Greatest Battles" was among his personal videos. He slid the disc into the player and turned it on with a remote, then moved to a window with a view of the dock. He pulled the heavy curtains back and opened the windows. Then he saw Tim searching the yard. Simon knew he'd head for the dock at any second and he turned the VCR's volume control up to the loudest. When Tim gave up searching the yard and started for the pier, Simon pushed the PLAY switch.

The real Crusher's gravely, booming voice blasted from giant stereo speakers with such powerful intensity that the window glass rattled. "Hi there, Crusher fans. Get ready for slam, bam, blood on the mat wrestling action from yours truly..."

Simon saw Tim freeze. Bewildered, he spun seeking the source of the incongruous hype. When he began running for the house, the boy dashed from the theater room and retreated to a rear door off the kitchen. Passing by the pantry he grabbed a plastic half-liter bottle of fruit juice, jammed it in his jacket pocket and left the house. He checked the yard and shore area. No Tim. As Crusher's voice boomed across the front yard, Simon ran for the dock.

Tim burst into the entertainment center. On the huge

screen he saw The Crusher slamming the head of a semiconscious opponent against a steel ring post. "The kid did this, but why?" He turned off the TV, glanced out the window in the direction of the dock and found his answer. Simon was running down the stone steps clutching his bow and arrows.

Racing along the main hall Tim passed by Jennifer's display cases of north coast Native American art. The Russian trade axe caught his eye. He stopped to draw his Swiss Army knife from his jeans. Holding it in a fist he swung the blunt end against the case and shattered the glass. He jumped back to avoid the shards falling around his feet, grabbed the Russian hand axe and sprinted for the front door. The weight and heft of the ancient weapon felt good in his hand and he fingered the cutting edge. "Be damned, it's still sharp."

As Simon pounded along the dock's wooden planks he glanced over his shoulder to see Tim burst out of the house. When Simon saw the hatchet in his hand he gasped, stumbled, and almost fell. Clutching the bow and quiver, he raced along the dock for the canoe that sat upside down on the low sawhorses. Simon knew he couldn't possibly launch before Tim caught up with him, but there was no other way to escape. In desperate fear for his life the boy ran on.

CHAPTER TWENTY-ONE

With the canoe almost within reach, Simon took one last look down the dock expecting the axe Tim carried to be arcing downward for his skull. What he saw was his pursuer braking to a stop twenty yards behind him and staring across the inlet. Then he noted that Tim had the axe hidden behind his back and was raising his other hand to wave a greeting. The boy glanced toward open water, but didn't slow his dash for the canoe.

What had brought Tim to a halt caused Simon to smile. A surge of relief overwhelmed him. Wanting to cheer, but still afraid, he thought, "The alarm worked!"

With its bow throwing a spirited wake of white water the San Juan Islands Security patrol boat sped into the mouth of the deep inlet heading directly for the dock. Even a quarter mile off Simon could see the two men in the big Boston Whaler and one was scanning the island through binoculars. He knew about "Murphy's Law" and decided not to chance that everything would go well now. He'd escape Tim first, and then flag down the security guys when they left the island, "They have guns and even

Tim couldn't fool them."

With a final glance at Tim who was smiling his good buddy grin at the approaching patrolmen, Simon rolled the canoe off the sawhorses and threw the bow and arrow quiver into the bottom. Using every once of fear-driven strength he shoved it across the dock. He gave himself a pat on the back for putting the paddle in the hull earlier. With a determined all-out push Simon slid the canoe into the water and leaped aboard. As the boy paddled off he looked back at Tim and saw him toss the axe into the sloop's cockpit and then ready a dock line to help tie up the oncoming patrol boat.

A hundred yards from the dock Simon laid down his paddle and put on a life vest. Though afraid, he was compelled to turn and look for Tim. Even at that distance the boy felt his cold murderous stare. He knew without a doubt that Tim would soon be after him.

The security officers in the Boston Whaler were so intent on their mission that they only gave Simon a fleeting glance as they sped by him for the dock.

Ernie, who was skippering the Boston Whaler, saw Tim's friendly wave and pulled back the throttles. He turned to his young partner. "You're probably right, it's a false alarm. We'll have a look see anyway, just in case."

"You mind if we make this fast?"

"I mind if we don't do our job. And, wasn't that Greenlee's kid in the canoe", said Ernie glancing over his shoulder at the boy.

"Must have been. Nice day for a paddle."

"Smart kid, he's wearing a life vest," the skipper remarked.

@

172

Two hundred yards off the dock, Simon lifted the paddle to catch his breath and rest his arms. He turned to watch the patrol boat nudge against the pier. He saw Tim wrap a dock line around a cleat and then shake hands with the uniformed security guards stepping off the Boston Whaler. Simon considered his next move as he watched Tim lead the two men off the pier toward the house. "Yeah, and he'll be smiling all the time he lies to them."

Making up his mind to forget any help from San Juan Islands Security, Simon resumed paddling for the headland. "Maybe Tim will bullshit them long enough for me to get around the point. And then what? Okay, I'm out of Tim's sight there. When the security guys leave they'll pass near me. I'll wave my jacket. It's rescue orange. They'll stop for sure."

Twenty minutes later, with aching arms, Simon reached the headland and looked across the strait to the island on the opposite side. With hardly a breeze, the water was still calm and he could see the low hills of San Juan Island far to the west. But his planned destination was much closer. Across the wide passage he could just make out the rustic cabins and small pier of Yeager's salmon fishing resort. The skiffs were tied to the dock, which meant that the guides had no city fisherman clients today, and someone would be there. He knew old man Yeager had a radio and he could call for the police and the security guys from there. He'd be safe if he could make the long paddle before the wind came up,

The boy took time to rest. Drifting along the shore off the headland he opened the bottle of juice he'd stuck in his jacket pocket. The infusion of liquid and fruit sugar quickly restored his energy, but did not ease his hunger, "With six of Belle's pecan cookies I bet I could make it across in half an hour."

At the thought of Belle he felt sadness rising. He desperately missed her and wanted to tell her about everything that had happened since Tim betrayed them. Picking up the paddle he thought, "I've got to make it to Yeager's. It's no big deal. Just a mile. Then I'll call the police and get Belle back. I swear I will."

As the San Juan Security patrolmen climbed aboard the Boston Whaler Tim thanked them for coming so quickly. They had believed his story about Simon sneaking into his father's work area and accidentally triggering the silent alarm. Ernie said it was a good day for a fast run and cautioned Tim, "You'd better tell the boy to let you know before he goes in there again."

The patrolman turned to look out the inlet. The boy was nowhere in sight. "The kid's gone around the point. Maybe we'd better check on him as well."

Tim felt a stab of panic and quickly said, "Don't bother. Simon paddles around the headland all the time. If I don't see him in a few minutes I'll fire up the Chris-Craft and go after him. Hell, I'll do it anyway, the engine needs to be run."

"Won't take you long in that boat," remarked the younger man, happy to be returning to Friday Harbor in time to catch the ferry to Seattle.

They shook hands again. Tim thanked the guards and the security patrol men boarded the Whaler. As they powered out of the inlet Tim waved good-bye and walked along the dock to the sloop. When he was sure they were on their way he exploded into action and dropped into the sailboat to retrieve the hand axe, then sprinted for the boathouse.

In less than a minute Tim had the Chris-Craft's engine started and the doors facing the inlet open. With the throttle jammed full forward he sent the speedboat blasting out of its berth for open water. Racing across the inlet he felt a growing sense of exhilaration and thought, "After I take care of Simon I'm out of here and on my way. Canada first. I'll take the skiff. It won't be conspicuous. Too bad about Christa. I was getting to like her."

Simon took a swallow of fruit juice, capped the bottle, and picked up the paddle. As he pointed the canoe's bow into the strait he saw the San Juan Security boat speeding out of the inlet and heading back for Friday Harbor. He stood in the canoe and frantically waved his orange jacket. The Boston Whaler raced away. With cry of anguish Simon realized that neither of the two men had noticed him.

Simon overcame his despair and paddled into the open water of the passage. Beyond the headland he felt a cool westerly breeze off the Pacific on his face. That wasn't good, but he figured he'd make it across before the whitecaps started. A hundred yards off the point he could see the mouth of the inlet and looked back at the island. He instantly recognized the pounding Chris-Craft charging directly for him. Simon realized he'd never make it to Yeager's and thought, "Maybe he'll let me go, or kidnap me until Dad pays ransom. That's bullshit. He'll kill me for sure."

A cold fearful certainty gripped Simon. He knew there was only one direction left for him. With a deep thrust of his paddle he turned the canoe around and sent it swiftly toward the island's rocky shore. Then the snarling noise of the Chris-Craft's engine bombarded Simon and he looked over his shoulder. He saw the speedboat swing round the headland and come racing directly at him. He paddled harder, desperately seeking shallow water where the big boat couldn't reach him. He chanced another glance back.

Tim had the speedboat on a certain collision course for the canoe.

He looked ahead searching for a way to escape. He was nearing shore, where a rocky outcropping showed above the water. With hard stabbing motions of the paddle Simon angled the canoe for the safety of the shoaling rocks and cobble beach beyond.

Heedless of the shallow water, and intent on running Simon over, Tim aimed the speedboat at the boy. An unseen rock scraped the wooden bottom of the boat and he saw the reef rising off the bow. As his left hand pulled back the throttle he spun the wheel sending the Chris-Craft skittering sideways, but not soon enough. At nearly full speed, the sleek mahogany hull slammed onto the jagged rocks.

The sharp outcropping ripped through the wooden planks, tearing the bottom open. The boat careened on until the bow smashed into a major upthrusting rock and came to an abrupt stop. As the boat's keel and ribs shattered, Tim was thrown violently forward against the instrument panel. His forehead cracked the tachometer's glass cover and the severe blow knocked him unconscious.

The violent grinding noise of the boat breaking up snapped Simon out of his fear-driven paddling. He glanced back and was astonished. What was left of the Chris-Craft was scattered amid the rocks. He could see Tim's head lying against the gunwale and that there was blood flowing down his face. Simon found himself giggling as he thought, "Dad's really going to be pissed about his boat."

Then the bow of the canoe scraped against the cobbles and Simon climbed out to begin dragging it ashore. When he was sure the canoe was above high tide line, the boy stopped to rest and looked back at the wreck of the Chris-Craft. Tim was as he last saw him; slumped unconscious and bleeding from the forehead. Simon thought about picking up a rock and, in case he was still alive, smashing his head in.

"After what he did, it would serve him right."

Then Tim's bloody head began to rise and next a hand appeared to grasp the gunwale. A moment later the boy saw Tim wipe the blood from his eyes and look directly at him. He seemed dazed, but his eyes held on Simon. When Tim began to struggle out of the shattered cockpit Simon grabbed his bow and quiver of arrows from the canoe. Taking a last look at Tim, who was now climbing out of the boat, he dashed for the tree line and plunged into the dense forest.

Still dazed and in terrible pain, Tim slid out of the boat and fell amid the rocks. The cold water and the sting of salt in his head wound shocked him back to the moment. "The boy, I've got to get the boy."

He started across the rocks for the shore and sensed he had forgotten something. It was the hand axe. He returned to the Chris-Craft, searched in the wreck of the cockpit, and found the weapon. When Tim reached dry land and stopped to rest beside the canoe he thought. "It would be just like that kid to lead me into the woods and then double back for the canoe. Little prick, you've got no canoe now."

In a fury, Tim flipped the canoe over and swung the axe, battering hole after hole though the frail bottom. The exertion caused his head to throb. He cursed the kid and glanced about. Checking his watch he muttered, "Shit, it'll be dark soon."

Wiping away the blood that dripped into his eyes, Tim plunged into the tall cedars. He had no difficulty picking up Simon's footprints, which showed clearly in the damp spongy soil. He followed the boy's track into the forest and started off among the towering trees.

Simon knew he had to elude Tim until dark. When night came he would find a place to hide. It would be cold, but hiding would allow him to live through the night, "But what about tomorrow? Okay, tomorrow I'll double back and get the canoe. It'll be calm then and I'll paddle to Yeager's."

He forced himself deeper into the dim tangle of the island's temperate rain forest. Images of old movies he had seen on television began to flow from his memory. Hawkeye in "Last of the Mohicans" escaped the Huron trackers by fleeing along a stream to conceal his footprints. The leader of Rogers Rangers in "Northwest Passage" got away from the Iroquois by leading his men into a cold swift river. The Rangers were so starved they ate their dead. And didn't he have a bow and quiver of arrows like Hawkeye? That thought gave him a flicker of confidence until he remembered that Tim, like the Huron and Iroquois, had a tomahawk. Simon also recalled that Tim kept his Swiss Army Knife in a pants pocket, "Will he scalp me alive?"

With growing panic, Simon looked about wildly for a stream. That was easy. Dozens of little creeks coursed down from the island's crown to find their way to the salt water. First he jumped on a rock, then another, and then stepped into a narrow brook. Cold water filled his tennis shoes and soaked his sox, making walking up the streambed difficult.

He glanced about and saw one of the 'No Hunting' signs he and Tim had posted only six days ago. He paused to regard the placard. The reminder of Tim's cruel betrayal almost brought him to tears. Fighting off despair, the boy scrambled up the stream bed, slipping on the moss again and again, He wasn't sure where he was going, but he had to find a place to hide. Like the desperate hunted animal he was becoming, Simon plunged ahead into raw nature.

Tim lost Simon's footprints where they vanished at the edge of the stream. He figured the boy would be following it into the island's interior to conceal his tracks. "He'll have to step out at some point, but what's his plan? He's smart, so be alert. Damn, my head hurts."

He stopped to bathe his wound with cold water and take a drink. As Tim brought his lips to the stream he caught sight of the bear's paw print. The depression was beginning to fill with water. The bear must have passed by only minutes ago. He stood, cautiously looked about, and thought, "Come on old bear. Find that kid for me. Just one really hard paw to his head and I'll donate a million to Bears Forever."

After a long careful inspection of the tangle of trees and ferns, Tim continued tracking along the stream. Even though the light was fading, the bent tips of fiddle ferns growing by the water told him Simon was still fleeing up the stream. He hurried on, head throbbing with pain, following the watercourse.

Simon was forced to stop where the stream suddenly became a mini-waterfall that fell through a cleft of jumbled rocks. He looked for a path that would allow him to remain in the water, but it was either scale the vertical rock wall or hike around it. He decided to chance leaving footprints and left the stream to circle the falls. The rocky escarpment continued on the other side and he was again able to conceal his tracks.

Then a wide clearing opened up before him. He paused to look around. On the other side of the open space, beyond a large fallen tree, the dense forest thrust upward again. Before crossing he dropped down and lay prone. Like a hunted animal, he used all his senses trying to locate his pursuer. He stared in the direction he had come and listened to the faint sounds of the forest. The breeze and the motion of cedar bows scraping together masked the footfalls he was trying to hear. He waited another minute, allowing the encompassing forest to soothe him, and finished the last of the fruit drink. He knew he'd be hungry later, but he wouldn't go thirsty on this island.

As his rapid breathing slowed Simon decided it was safe to proceed. He hid the bottle and cautiously dashed across the open space. He chanced a glance back. There was Tim. His attention was focused on the ground and before he looked up Simon sprinted for the forest beyond. He reached the fallen tree and leaped over the wide slippery trunk. He lost his balance, landed hard, and was momentarily dazed, but was well aware Tim was approaching. Had he seen him? Should he run for the trees? If he did flee, Tim would certainly spot him. If he stayed behind the log he'd be caught and killed, "Where's Tim now?"

Keeping low, Simon crawled along the trunk to the wider butt end and chanced a peek across the clearing. Tim stood there staring at the woods beyond. The blood seeping from his head wound made him appear even more fearsome. And the axe Simon feared dangled from his right hand. He knew there was no way he could escape now. Like a cornered animal, Simon knew he had to fight back or die. Withdrawing behind the massive, rotting tree trunk the boy pulled two arrows from the quiver and notched one to the bow's string.

Tim spotted Simon's tracks where they started across the clearing and began following them. As he moved closer to the fallen log a slight blur of color showing along the ridge of the trunk caused him to pause. He squinted and recognized that the orange tint came from the cloth of Simon's Patagonia windbreaker. With a feeling of elation Tim charged after Simon.

CHAPTER TWENTY-TWO

Tim's sudden sprint displaced twigs and gravel creating a grating sound that alerted Simon. The boy had to know where his attacker was. He slipped the quiver of arrows off his shoulder so they wouldn't rattle and alert Tim. Then Simon cautiously peered over the log. Tim was almost on top of him and holding the axe ready to strike. In the second that remained before the man could drive the blade into his skull Simon drew the bow string full back and, without hesitating to aim, released the arrow.

The steel point struck Tim between his heart and right shoulder with sufficient power to drive the arrow deep into his pectoral muscle. The arrow's forceful impact stopped him. Astonished, he stared wide-eyed at Simon, who was as shocked by the outcome as Tim. Before Simon could notch the second arrow, Tim raised the hand axe. Simon spun and ran for the tree line.

Even with the arrow deep in his upper chest, Tim managed to crawl over the log. Then, as Simon had, he slipped on the moss-slick bark and fell. His impact on the ground caused the embedded arrow to twist. As muscle fiber tore he roared with pain.

At the sound of Tim's cry the boy looked back and saw him lying on the ground. When the trees enveloped Simon he moved behind a cedar and stopped to catch his breath. He could still see Tim. He was struggling to a sitting position. After a painful effort he was able to rest his back against the log. Simon thought about rushing Tim and finishing him off with another arrow. Then he realized that the quiver was back at the log and he had only the single arrow in his hand. If he shot from any distance beyond ten yards he might miss. Then it would be all over. Maybe Tim wouldn't rise to pursue him. Maybe his arrow had entered his heart and he would fall dead any minute. Simon remained behind the tree watching, waiting, silently hoping that Tim would die right there.

Enduring excruciating pain, Tim grasped the arrow's shaft and pulled it out of his chest. He watched with disbelief as blood spurted from the wound staining his sweatshirt crimson. He jammed a finger over the puncture to stop the flow and tried to think of what to do next. After two minutes of direct pressure he removed his hand and found that the bleeding had slowed, "And I talked Greenlee into buying that bow for camp parents day."

Moving cautiously to avoid opening the wound Tim reached for his knife and cut off his sweatshirt. Next, he wrapped the fabric around his chest and folded the leftover cotton into a compress which he slid under the bandage and over the puncture. Satisfied he had stopped the bleeding, Tim got to his feet. Feeling lightheaded, he swayed and put a hand on the log to steady himself. Then he spotted Simon's quiver of arrows. He leaned them against the fallen tree and, one-by-one, broke them in half with his foot. Each jolt of his leg against an arrow brought searing pain.

Simon had seen enough. He knew Tim would soon be after him. The boy dropped down on his hands and knees and crept away. When he was sure Tim wouldn't see him, Simon came to his feet and dashed on looking for another stream to conceal his tracks. He quickly found a small creek and started upward. A dim memory from an old war movie on TV came rushing out of his brain along with the hero's dialog, "We've got to take the high ground. We can stop 'em from the ridge."

"Maybe I can get a real close shot from above," Simon thought, "Maybe I can put one in his eye. But he'd still have one left."

The stream's cold water chilled Simon and he began to shiver. He pulled the orange jacket's zipper to his chin and waded upward. A mound of rocks blocked his way, but this clump was climbable. He crawled over the slippery boulders. He reached a high spot and looked back to search for Tim. But it wasn't Tim that brought a stab of fear. The bear was twenty yards in front of Simon stripping blackberries from a tangle of vines. Before the boy could retreat, the bear caught his scent and stood tall to peer at the intruder. As he had seen Tim do, Simon began talking softly to the bear. "It's okay, bear. I'm going. Those berries are all yours. See you, bear."

Leaving the stream bed, he slowly backed away murmuring, "Good bear. Eat those blackberries."

The bear dropped to all fours and returned to feeding.

Some sixty yards below Simon, in the tangle of forest and ferns, Tim heard Simon's distant voice, "Good bear. Eat those blackberries."

He gaged Simon's direction as easily as the bear caught the boy's scent and hurried up the slope. Even in the fading light he found Simon's footprints and, despite his pain and dizziness, he forced himself upward.

The area appeared familiar. Fifty yards further on the trees opened up and he found himself at the small lake where the salmon were spawning. The Chinook were there in a thick mass, dorsal fins showing, bodies and hooked jaws grossly deformed in preparation for their pre-death mating ritual.

He wanted to pause, rest beside them, and watch the dying males deposit their seed among the female's eggs. "Later I can do that. Later I can have my own salmon stream. Business first, Tim. Take care of business. Go for broke. Win this one and you can have your own island, twenty times bigger than Greenlee's."

With a final look at the mating salmon, Tim moved on. He was feeling weak, but shook it off.

Two hundred yards beyond the lake Simon stopped his retreat where the river cascaded down the steep gorge toward the strait. He stared at the rotten log that spanned the chasm, remembering what had happened when he tried to cross it before. How many days ago was that? Five days? A week? His sense of time had been drained away by the trauma of the last few hours. He turned to look back. He knew that Tim was surely behind him, and wounded or not he was coming.

Simon thought, "I bet I've lost at least five pounds. It'll hold my weight." He took a deep breath and stepped onto the thick, slippery cedar trunk and started across. He recalled a TV show about a tightrope walker. The daredevil had cautioned never look down. Always look ten feet ahead. The old decaying log began to sag and Simon held his eyes on the far side of the gorge.

A short distance beyond the lake, Tim arrived at the gorge, and remembered, "Yeah, I was here with the kid and Belle. And there's that log Simon almost fell off."

The roaring flow of water cascading from the lake and down the

184

narrow defile beat into Tim's brain. The jumble of hissing, splashing sounds confused him. He stopped before the decaying cedar trunk that spanned the crevasse and leaned on the butt end to rest. His eyes searched the underbrush beyond. "The kid still has an arrow. Better not be a sitting target."

He moved along the edge of the steep water-filled gorge looking for signs of the boy. A few yards from the fallen tree he found Simon's footprints and followed them until they disappeared amid the rock rubble at the base of the rotten trunk that spanned the gorge. "Be damned. He crossed over. Or did he? Now I have to take a chance."

CHAPTER TWENTY-THREE

Before stepping onto the fallen tree Tim carefully searched the tangled forest on the far side of the gorge. His growing feeling of desperation was reinforced by the ache in his head and the throbbing pain from the arrow's wound. The light was almost gone and he suspected that the boy was hiding in wait for him like a cornered animal. He had to find the kid. If he didn't, and Simon was alive when the Greenlees returned tomorrow, it was all over. He could head for Canada in the skiff, and then on to the Far East as planned, but if he was caught, the boy's testimony would hang him.

Tim moved a few yards upstream for a better view. For a long moment he stared into the dense stand of cedars. Nothing. He moved on thinking about the rotten tree. If he crossed quickly, stepping lightly, he figured it would take his weight. Only five days ago it had supported him and Simon. But did the boy cross or not? Then his eyes caught a slight hint of orange deep within the foliage on the other side of the gorge. "Got you now, kid."

Moving slowly, Tim returned to the fallen tree. He touched his wound and the pain snapped him back into sharp focus on what he must do. He had to act now, or forever give up what he had planned so long for. His hand tightened on the axe. He'd charge the kid. And in the thick brush it was unlikely Simon could draw the bow to get a clean shot at him.

Tim stepped onto the log and started across the gorge. He felt the spongy slick trunk begin to sag. He suppressed the urge to sprint the rest of the way and continued his cautious, deliberate pace. At mid-point from his higher elevation he again caught sight of Simon's orange jacket. It was draped over a low tree limb. He knew then that Simon had placed it there to lure him across, "Go on. There's no turning back."

From behind came Simon's calm, emotionless voice, "Bet you don't make it across."

Tim froze and fought down rising panic. He looked cautiously over his shoulder and saw Simon standing on the bank holding the fully drawn bow. Then, through the soles of his hiking boots, Tim felt the decaying trunk begin to splinter. He had to make his move and right now. As if walking on a mine field, he carefully turned to face the boy.

He saw Simon aiming the arrow at his face. There was no mistaking his intent. Tim knew the boy wouldn't miss at this close range and readied the axe to hurl. Forcing his good buddy smile, he thought about offering a deal or pleading that he had saved the boy from the same log. Simon's look of determination said that was impossible. He must kill him no matter what. As he raised his arm to hurl the tomahawk the rotten log crumbled and snapped in half. Tim made a desperate lunge to grasp the rim of the gorge and the axe fell from his hand. Dropping into the chasm he reached out to save himself. Below the rock ledge his hands gripped a projecting tree root. He dangled there and then his left foot found a toehold.

Overcoming the searing pain of his wound Tim struggled upward. His right hand found a solid grip, as did both of his feet. Taking a deep breath, he set himself to spring over the edge. Where was the boy? He had to know. Tim clawed upward and hooked one hand onto solid rock. He looked over the rim. Simon was standing directly above him. The steel point of the arrow was two feet from his face. He would either die from the arrow or plunge to his death. Tim had one other choice. He begged for his life, "Simon, please. I saved you once. Save me." He watched the boy move cautiously closer to the edge and pleaded, "The bow. Let me grab it."

Simon's unblinking eyes held on Tim and the boy began to tremble as if consumed by an inner demon. Simon felt dizzy and shut his eyes momentarily. He saw himself standing with Tim on the log that had just fallen. He was Simon's good buddy then, carrying him off the rotten trunk, saving his life.

Then into his nightmare of conflicts came mind flashes of Tim's shooter game. He saw the animated stick figure of his father turning to raise his hands in surrender and heard the shooter's gun firing. With absolute flash photo clarity he visualized his father's avatar flung backwards from the bullet's impact.

"Simon, please..."

The boy returned from the agony of his regression to the edge of the gorge and Tim's terrified plea. He then became conscious of his painful fingers locked on the arrow and bow string. Simon opened his eyes and saw Tim reaching out for him. He released the tension on the bow string and allowed the arrow to fall. Taking a deep breath, Simon extended the bow for Tim to grasp, and then slowly drew it back out of the man's reach.

Time stopped for man and boy. Tim made a final lunge, attempting to grab Simon's ankles. The boy was quicker and leaped back to escape Tim's hand. Tim's sudden violent movement caused the ground to break up around him. A microsecond later the loose soil gave way. Amid the cascading earth Tim tumbled backward into the gorge.

Simon watched Tim fall. His head hit a rock abutment and he careened into the rushing water. The narrow swift flowing river quickly carried his limp body down the steep gorge and out of sight. Simon took a final look over the edge to make sure Tim was truly gone and thought, "That was for Belle and Christa."

Physically exhausted and emotionally devastated, Simon picked up his bow and the remaining arrow. With the sound of water plunging down the gorge hammering at him Simon turned away. At last the tears he had held back for so long began to flow. Bear or not, he started for home.

At the edge of the lake Simon stopped to rest. He was thirsty and cupped his hands to scoop up a drink. Suddenly, the water erupted in front of him and he saw a large male salmon twisting around a female Chinook. He knew they were mating and wanted to stay to watch them, but darkness was coming and he hurried off. Down the hill he came to the fallen log where he had dropped the quiver of arrows and discovered that Tim had broken them all. He slung the empty quiver over his shoulder and walked on.

Simon crossed the headland as the last light of day cast a pink glow over the deep inlet. He could clearly see his home and the dock. Weary beyond belief he sat on a rock to rest. Simon's gaze fell on the sloop and he thought that he would take his father sailing, and they'd really talk, like he'd talked with Belle. They'd talk about Tim and what had happened. He promised himself he'd tell his dad about hacking the company credit card number, even if his father already knew.

The exhausted boy felt he was safe now and took time to watch the sunset before walking the last half mile home. He told himself he should call the police, but was too emotionally drained to face that or anything else except finding something to eat and going to sleep.

Sharp clicking sounds interrupted his thoughts and he directed his gaze to the thick kelp bed spread across the glass-smooth water below the headland. Simon's curiosity was peaked and he searched for the source of the unusual tapping. Movement among the kelp fronds caught his attention. The sea otters were still there. In the dimness he could just make out what was causing the clicking noise. The pair of otters were floating on their backs amid the thick mat of kelp.

They held rocks in their forepaws and were hammering open butter clams that rested on their chests. He was entranced by their resourcefulness and the speed with which they devoured the clam flesh. Then one of the otters reached out and snatched a clam from the other. A mock fight ensued and they gave up feeding to chase each other through the kelp forest. The boy laughed at their exuberant play and the sound of his own voice startled him.

He entered the dark house by the kitchen door. Before turning on the lights he stood just inside the threshold listening for sounds of movement. In the black silence he clutched the bow tightly and imagined that Tim might have survived, might have returned. Simon knew that was impossible, but the fear was there. Overcoming his dread, he flicked on the kitchen lights and hurried for the refrigerator. He slid open the freezer. Ice cream and frozen pecan cookies awaited him. Simon shook his head and closed the drawer. He rewarded his escape by reaching for an apple and a hunk of Swiss cheese, "When I see Belle again I'll tell her no more cookies."

Later, with his hunger appeased, Simon patrolled the house. Everything was as he had left it. In his father's work room he switched on the satellite link and held the phone to his ear. He heard the comforting dial tone and thought of calling the police. He wasn't ready yet to call or e-mail anyone. What had happened had numbed him. He shut down his father's computer, secured the work room door and slowly walked through the hush of the empty house. When Simon discovered his mother's smashed display case he found a broom and dustpan and swept up the glass shards.

On impulse, he picked up a large brightly painted Southern Kwakiutl salmon carving. He cradled the heavy sculpture in his arms and felt the spirit of the fish emerging from the ancient, though still aromatic cedar. His mother had told him that the carving had once sat on top of a totem pole to honor the salmon that had made life possible for the native peoples of the Northwest.

Simon pictured the Chinook swimming up the gorge and into the island lake. He remembered Tim's words about having a purpose and making sure the salmon survived. He didn't want to think about him anymore. He carefully put the carving back on its shelf. Tightly holding his bow and the single arrow, he wandered on through the soundless empty house.

He was jumpy and on edge. He peered inside the family theater room, looked at the giant TV set and shook his head. Television and videos were so remote from what he had gone through that they held no appeal. He entered his own room and sat down at the computer, but couldn't bring his hand to switch it on. Then he raised his eyes to stare at the wrestler's poster. He hated the man now. With sure deliberation, he climbed onto the desk and ripped the poster off the blond Port Orford cedar paneling. Simon's decisive act eased some of his melancholy. He again thought about calling the police and then e-mailing his parents. They were probably aboard a 747 and the cops would yammer at him for hours. He was too exhausted to handle it by himself. He needed his mother and father.

Before leaving his room Simon opened his closet and dug into the tangle of clothes, shoes and rain gear searching for a carton of twelve new target arrows. As he burrowed into the mess the bright overhead light revealed a slim plastic insulated wire that ran along the baseboard of the closet and then disappeared under the carpet. Why hadn't he noticed it before? And when was it installed? It was a mystery to Simon and he was too numb to solve it. He'd trace the wire tomorrow. He found the arrows, thumbed the sharp points, and filled the quiver. Leaving the jumble of the closet, Simon grabbed his bow and cautiously eased down the long, empty hall to Belle's room.

He opened her door and peered inside. The room smelled of Belle's scent and the flowers she always placed on the chest of drawers where sunlight coming in the window would highlight their delicate colors. He stepped inside and turned on her bedside light. In the lamp's soft glow he saw that the roses she had grown in the green house had wilted and their fallen petals covered the dresser top. He walked around the room, glanced at the photos of Belle's family, and then picked up a book, The Little Prince. It was the one she had urged him to read. He would read it. For her.

A profound sadness came welling up from his love for Belle. Without realizing what he was doing, the boy lay on the bed with the bow and arrows close beside him, and drew her down comforter over himself. Simon missed her terribly. He promised himself that he would somehow bring her back into his life. He drew Belle's pillow into his arms, hugging its softness, and his tears flowed until sleep eased his torment.

CHAPTER TWENTY-FOUR

Simon stood on the dock watching the sky and holding his bow and quiver. Since he awoke the weapon had never left his hand. He used the hours since waking in the empty silent house to find the skiff's fuel can and start the boat's outboard. Though he knew his parents wouldn't fly in until early afternoon, he had been waiting all morning for their return.

He still feared that Tim might have survived. If he had to flee the skiff would take him all the way to Friday Harbor. After Simon had started the outboard three times, and was certain he could run the boat, he gathered Tim's computer and hard drive and hid them. Simon knew his father would not want the story of his past dealings with Tim to go public.

His thoughts shifted to what he would tell his parents about Tim and all that had happened. "I'll tell them about the bear and the otters and that the salmon were spawning, and how Tim tried to kill me and how I tricked him." He wondered if he should reveal that Tim had once saved him from falling into the gorge. He decided he would. If his father ever bought another canoe, he'd paddle around the headland to the kelp beds and drift there with the otters. He was restless now and growing ever more impatient. Then Simon remembered the unfamiliar wire he had discovered last night.

What was it for and where did it lead?

@

What he had found last night in his closet was unexpected. Jammed below the edge of the carpet where it met the wall Simon fingered a very thin, fiber optic cable. He peeled back the carpet and followed the wire to where it disappeared into the base molding. Directly beyond was the main upstairs hallway. He left his room and discovered where the cable exited the baseboard and traced it along the hall where it was tucked into the edge of the carpet.

Tracking the cable downstairs, he followed it to the back of the house and into a storage pantry where the wire entered a pencil thin white plastic conduit and went underground. But where did it end? He looked out a kitchen window. Across the yard was the squat soundproof generator building. He hurried outside and ran for the power house. Simon felt light on his feet and noticed he wasn't breathing hard, "Either I've lost weight or I'm high on adrenalin."

In the powerhouse the constant hum of twin diesel generators and their intense electromagnetic field distracted the boy. For a moment he couldn't remember why he had come here. He wanted things to be like they were, especially Belle's friendship and his mother and father scolding him about spending too much time on the computer and urging him to cut down on sweets. He shook off his confusion and looked around the building's sparse interior until he found what he was seeking.

At floor level the slender fiber optic cable came out of its conduit and ran up the far wall into a large metal storage cabinet. He moved closer. The steel doors were secured by a padlock. He wanted inside. Something, some inner perception, said the contents of the cabinet were important. Looking around he spotted a large steel breaker bar that workmen had used to dig post holes through the rocky ground. He grasped the heavy metal rod and jammed the pointed end through the lock's hasp. Using all his strength, the boy pulled down on the bar. With the intense leverage he applied, the lock broke open. Simon drew the metal doors apart and looked inside. "Wow, what is all that stuff?"

He reached out and ran his fingers over a bank of ten digital video recorders that rested on metal racks. Green LED lights glowed indicating that the machines were in operation. Below the recorders were stacks of previously recorded DVDs, each with contents dated and precisely labeled in his father's neat printing... Boathouse, Simon's Room, Belle's Room, Guest Room, Kitchen, Dock, Studio... "He's got video of every room in the house. Why is he doing this?"

On another shelf were several cases of unused disks and a small box marked with the Sony logo that caught his attention. He opened the carton. Inside was a tiny digital video surveillance camera half the size of a woman's lipstick, "Doesn't he trust his own family?"

On impulse he turned off the recorders and began rapidly unloading tapes labeled with the current month and packed them in an empty carton. After loading fresh DVDs into the recorders he turned them on again, grabbed the discs he wanted, and hurried to the house.

Clutching the box of tapes, Simon eased into Christa's room. He had to know if a camera was hidden there and if there was a recording of what went on between Tim and Christa. His eyes flicked about searching for where a tiny lens might be concealed. He asked himself, "Where would I hide one so the whole room could be seen? Simon had a flash of insight, "Of course, in the smoke alarm."

His gaze held on white plastic cover fixed to the ceiling between the bed and desk. He had to make sure his reasoning was correct. He shoved the desk under the fixture, put a chair on top, and carefully climbed to the seat. He was now high enough to reach the plastic cover and pry it off the warning device. A micro camera was indeed there, a duplicate of the one he'd discovered in the powerhouse. Now he could learn what had happened in this room, and elsewhere in the house, since Tim's arrival. Had a camera caught Tim breaking into his father's office and forcing him to reveal the location of the motion sensor switch? Simon was sure it had been taped, "I've got to see it all."

Carrying the box of DVDs, Simon edged into the family entertainment center and locked the door. He clapped his hands twice and soft theater lights hidden behind a valance lit the room. At the far end a huge television set was built into the wall. Seven black leather Eames chairs were arranged in a semicircle facing the big screen. A wet bar with its refrigerator and espresso machine flanked a side wall. On the opposite side were racks of state of the art media systems capable of playing anything from ancient 78 RPM records to HS video cards.

Simon went right to the DVD player and inserted the disc labeled, "Boathouse". Then he settled into an Eames chair and picked up a remote control..

Onto the wide screen came a dim black and white image of the interior of the boathouse upstairs apartment. At first the picture was motionless like a grainy, out of focus photograph. Simon figured the camera was set to record at low resolution to allow a single disc to capture a week or more of visual data.

He held down the fast forward button until the exposure brightened and the figure of a man entered carrying two bundles wrapped in green plastic Simon gasped with fear, reliving his recent terror. "He's dead. He's got to be."

In seconds the accelerated images revealed Tim setting up a sophisticated laptop computer and attaching an external hard drive. The boy continued to fast forward until something about Greenlee Electronics appeared. He paused the image and tried to read what was on the screen. What he saw was a fuzzy copy of a newspaper story, but the focus was too soft to make out individual words, "Something about dad and his company."

He ran the video ahead until Tim was seen leaving the room. Simon inserted another DVD labeled 'Christa's room'.

His eyes widened as he watched the nude couple entwined in their passionate lovemaking. In awe he said aloud, "They're doing it." He wanted to watch longer, but his fascination was overcome by a desperate need to know about what really went on between Tim and Christa. He advanced the tape until they stopped their frenzied grappling and lay side by side to begin to talk. The boy turned up the volume and leaned forward, watching and listening to the couple with total absorption.

Christa was sweating and still panting as Simon heard her say, "You're one passionate lover, Tim."

"It's like we were made, or fated, for each other."

"And it's over for us in four more days."

Simon watched him run a finger along Christa's lips. As she kissed it he said, "Doesn't have to be."

"You're saying?"

"We both have dreams that can come true."

She looked away from him to the door, "As you said, right downstairs, only a locked door away."

"You said it now, Christa."

"Millions, even billions. But the risk. Who would take the chance?"

The boy watched Tim sit up to face her. His good natured smile was replaced by a hard, convincing reasonableness, "Powerful people in Singapore, Taiwan, Korea. We open Alex's door, they buy. Adios Greenlee Electronics. Hello, France, Fiji, South Africa. We get lost for awhile, surface, use what we have to build something else — bigger, useful, and have some fun along the way."

"You think big, Tim."

Simon watched Tim draw Christa close to him and kiss her breasts., "You're a very strong influence on me. Hell, we can have our own damned country, or a private island like this one, with a pier and a yacht, if you'd like."

She pulled back from him and said with surprise, "You're really serious."

"If you'd dare..."

"I want the power money brings, but I couldn't. It's just not in me to steal."

Simon saw Tim stiffen for an instant. Then he threw himself onto her and with a soft laugh said, "Well it was a fun thought."

Simon had seen enough. He turned off the video. At last he was able to accept that he was in no way responsible for Christa's death, "He had her jibe the boat so the boom would hit her, and then he let her drown. He really did, and he was going to kill me next."

200

Impulsively, Simon hid the DVDs in the little refrigerator beside the wet bar. Then he went to the picture window that overlooked the inlet and pulled the heavy drapes aside. "The plane's coming soon. Better go. I want to greet mom and dad."

He paced along the dock, looking eastward, hoping the plane would be early. The sight of a small fishing boat approaching the headland stopped his restless pacing. He went to the boathouse locker, opened it and pulled out the binoculars that he had left there after watching Christa sail away with Tim.

Through the magnification of the lenses he spotted two men in the skiff. They weren't hunters this time. Even at a half mile off he could see their fishing rods. Simon knew with absolute certainty that they were planning to land at the river mouth where the salmon were gathering in the shallows and couldn't be caught from a boat. They'd fish from shore, on his island, and he couldn't allow that. With rising anger driving him, Simon grabbed his bow and began running to intercept them.

This time the island's interior held no fear for Simon. He knew the way to the river mouth and what to do if he should encounter the bear. He arrived out of breath to find the fishermen already casting salmon lures. He hid behind a wide cedar listening to the anglers calling excitedly to each other. Simon felt violated. He notched an arrow to the bow string and silently moved from hiding. The men were so absorbed by the mass gathering of Chinook that they failed to notice Simon step from the trees.

When he was ten yards from the two men the boy called, "No fishing allowed here."

The surprised pair spun to see the boy holding the drawn bow. There was no mistaking his intensity or that the arrow was aimed at them. When one started to speak, Simon cut him off, "This is my island and

I'm asking you just once to leave the way you came."

One of the men took a step forward. Simon released the arrow and it zinged between them. He had another drawn and ready to fire before the startled men could react. They exchanged glances, picked up their fishing gear and walked to their skiff. When Simon was certain they weren't trying to trick him he released the bow string and thought, "Wow, did I really do that?"

Simon watched the men launch the skiff and then returned to the dock. He picked up the binoculars and saw that the fishermen's boat was on a heading across the strait. He figured they wouldn't come back today.

He sat down on the dock beside the still water to wait. As the sun warmed him Simon's tension from the confrontation drained away. He felt truly at peace, like he belonged on the island. He ran his fingers over the coarse wood planks. The rough texture and intricate grain of the fir decking absorbed his attention. The beauty of the salt and sun weathered wood brought a smile as he began to understand why his father cherished the island's trees. Then Simon remembered that it was an old decaying cedar log that had spared his life and taken Tim's.

The faint, far off sound of an aircraft engine began to rise and Simon stood to search the sky. To the east the distant profile of a floatplane appeared and he recognized the engine's deep, steady throb. A minute later the familiar blue and white aircraft began descending for the inlet. Instead of landing, the old Beaver flew directly over Simon and then banked steeply to circle the dock. Simon looked up at the fuselage windows and saw his father and mother waving at him. He lifted the bow high overhead and pumped it up and down to welcome them home. In the aft window he noticed someone else. It was Belle. And she was smiling.

CHAPTER TWENTY-FIVE

Simon was surprised to see Casper Graham squeeze through the floatplane's cabin door. Overweight and usually wheezing, the Greenlee family attorney rarely visited the island unless there was some sort of legal emergency involving his father. As they all rushed for Simon the boy thought, "I bet what happened yesterday will really freak them out."

After hugs and inspecting Simon to make sure he was alright, they started for the house. Alex was the first ask his son a direct question, "Where's Tim?"

"He's dead. Or at least I hope he is."

"Very funny, Simon."

"I'm serious Dad."

With rising alarm Jennifer asked, "And Christa?"

"He killed her."

At that sudden unexpected news the adults exchanged shocked glances. Belle was the first to move and she placed her hands protectively on Simon's shoulders. Before they could bombard Simon with questions the lawyer lowered himself to the boy's eye level and said casually, "I think we'd better calmly discuss everything that went on here while your parents were away. And most important, Simon. Did you call the police or tell anyone what happened?"

"No. I didn't talk to anyone. I thought mom and dad should know first."

"That was very wise, Simon."

Graham faced Alex and Jennifer. "So let's give Simon as much space and time as he needs to tell us what happened right from the beginning. After we decide on how to slant this, I'll call the police on your behalf."

The lawyer saw the tension drain from the boy's parents and thought, "Casper, you will soon be earning every dollar your firm has over-charged the Greenlees these past five years."

Simon took Belle's hand and they all walked up the wide steps to the house. She leaned close to the boy and whispered, "Are you truly alright, Simon?"

He whispered back. "I'm okay, now that I know you're okay. But I'm really hungry."

He saw she was crying. Her tears brought his own. His feeling of love for her, his mother and father, the sea otters playing in the kelp and even their patient, understanding lawyer, gave Simon a clear insight into what he must do before the day was over. He wiped his cheeks and hurried after Jennifer and Alex and the lawyer.

Simon handed Casper Graham the business card the older detective had given him and the lawyer made his call to the police. As Graham waited for the detective he turned to Simon, "You could have called them last night. They'll ask you about that."

"I'll tell them I was too traumatized."

The lawyer nodded an okay and thought, "This might go better than I expected."

When Simon finished his detailed account and excused himself to pee, Jennifer remarked, "He's lost weight."

Alex had another observation, "And his voice is changing. He didn't squeak once."

Belle laughed inwardly, "Ah, tres bien. He'll be a handsome young man one day and find a girl to love."

After the two detectives finished questioning Simon and his parents their attorney summarized the facts surrounding Christa's and Tim's deaths, and the disappearance of Karl Mannheim. Then they discussed Tim's motivation for killing Christa and attempting to murder Simon. The detectives agreed that the boy was in no way responsible for either death, but they needed to dig deeper to learn the why of Tim's brutal actions and how Simon's father was involved.

Simon knew exactly why. He had hidden Tim's laptop and hard drive. The motivation was all there. It was his secret. His leverage.

Lawyer Graham carefully explained that Tim was a disgruntled computer programmer who irrationally believed that Alex Greenlee had stolen his work. The officers seemed to buy the lawyer's reasoning and said they would do a background check on the man.

It was enough for now that the authorities knew Tim had a smoldering, long standing grievance against Simon's father. Then the lawyer made his plea to the detectives to temporarily keep Christa's murder and Tim's presumed accidental death from the media. The older policeman offered, "If some snoop digs deep enough its all going to come out. So, no promises but we'll do what we can within the law."

The younger detective turned to Simon. "Why didn't you tell us about that guy when we were out here before? We could have arrested him right then."

"He made me feel like I was responsible for Christa's death 'cause I didn't get the canoe out there soon enough."

Simon sensed his father intently watching him and thought, "I've got to talk with Dad alone and soon."

The senior detective cautioned the Greenlees that the police might have further questions and not to make any travel plans without checking with them first. He also advised the family that a police forensic investigator would be arriving tomorrow and not to disturb anything that might be considered evidence in the case. "And we'll dispatch the dive team to search for the body."

The detectives left aboard the Friday Harbor police launch and the Greenlee's attorney flew back to Seattle on the floatplane. Graham had urged that he must give the Dutch Phillips/Greenlee merger a final review and would return with the contract tomorrow. Simon, his parents and Belle walked the lawyer to the plane and said their good-byes. As the old Beaver took off, Alex turned to his son and raised his voice to carry over the roar of the engine, "When all this is settled, we'll have our own plane. Want to learn how to fly with me?"

"Like pilot and copilot. You know, sort of like partners?"

Alex sensed that his son was hinting at something, "What are you getting at Simon?"

"Dad, I want to take you to where it all happened, so you'll really understand."

Alex looked down at Simon, saw that his son was deadly serious, and nodded. The boy brightened and quickly added, "We'll need to use the skiff since he wiped out the Chris-Craft and smashed the canoe. And he hid the outboard's fuel tank but I found it and hooked it up this morning. The motor started just fine." He saw his father's inquisitive look and added, "I needed to know it would start, just in case he wasn't really dead and I had to make a run for it."

Alex noted that the boy had avoided saying Tim's name. And why go by boat when they could walk? He sensed that Simon had an unconscious need to find Tim's body for a final closure to all the terror he had undergone. He held his questions back. "Sure. I'll run the skiff and you navigate. When do you want to go?"

"As soon as I get my bow and arrows. And you'd better get some warm clothes on."

Alex laughed to himself, "Now he's taking charge."

@

As the skiff passed by the headland Simon had desperately paddled around the day before he scanned the water hoping to see Tim's body. His father noticed his attention shift from shore to sea. Alex understood what Simon was searching for and idled the outboard motor. Standing side by side they slowly drifted toward the nearby rocks. The splintered wreck of the Chris-Craft was still strewn about the cobble beach along last night's high tide line. Alex shook his head, "He really did a job on my boat."

"He was going almost full speed for me when he hit the rocks."

207

"Well, too bad he wasn't going a little faster. He might not have survived."

Simon nodded and pointed to the wreck. "Just to the right of the boat there's a bit of gravel beach where we can land."

"Anything else I need to know, Simon?"

"Like could he be alive and waiting for us? No way he's alive. Not after what happened."

"But you'd like to know for sure."

"Wouldn't you?"

Alex sensed that Simon's last remark held a hidden meaning and thought, "What the hell kind of game is he playing?"

Holding his bow and shouldering the quiver of arrows, Simon led his father through the shallows to the wreck. He pointed out where the blood from Tim's head wound had dried on the varnished wood of the cockpit combing. "He was so dazed it gave me time to get away. Maybe I should have killed him when I could have, but I was really spooked."

They paused at the battered canoe and turned from the shore. Tim's and Simon's footprints still showed clearly in the damp muddy soil that flanked the stream. A quarter mile inland by the blackberries Simon spotted larger prints and pointed to the bear claw marks. He saw his father's look of deep concern.

"Don't worry, Dad. He taught Belle and me how to calm that bear so he wouldn't charge. Really. We'll be okay."

Behind the large cedar tree trunk that lay to the far side of the open meadow Alex picked up a handful of Simon's broken target arrows. He stared at the splintered wood with disbelief and turned to Simon, "And after you put an arrow in his shoulder you had only one left?"

"Yeah, and he taught me to shoot this bow you gave me. Kind of ironic isn't it Dad?"

Tim's trail allowed easy tracking and they followed his prints to the small lake where the Chinook were still spawning. They guessed Tim had stopped to rest by the dying salmon. Alex started to remark on the marvel they were watching, but Simon had the last word, "Really special, aren't they? And they left here as fingerlings three years ago."

Alex watched the salmon, thinking, "What else did Tim teach him?"

Five minutes later they were staring into the deep gorge. The swirling mist rising from the turbulent flow of the narrow river chilled them and they drew back from the roaring torrent. After Simon calmly described what had happened and how he had fooled Tim with his jacket, he led his father along the rim of the gorge. Simon sighed as he explained, "He was hanging onto a root to keep from falling. He begged me to save him and I stuck out my bow for him to grab. But I knew he would kill me. I drew it back and then he reached out to grab my ankle and I stepped back. The earth gave way and down he went."

He led his father to the ledge where the earth had given way and carried Tim into the rapids. There was no sign of a body. Simon sighed again. With a note of resignation he concluded, "I tricked him into going out on that log."

"You made the right decision, Simon."

"I had to."

"That's a tough lesson to learn."

"How did you learn to be tough, Dad?"

"Simon, you led me up here for a special reason. So how about we find a sunny spot beside the lake and you tell me what this is all about."

@

For almost three minutes Simon stared silently at the salmon growing ever more sluggish in their final hour. His father knew the boy was forming some sort of pronouncement and allowed him to take his time. Simon looked away from the lake and took a deep breath. Alex noticed how healthy his son looked and how capable he seemed, "And he's growing in tune with nature."

Alex's patience wore thin, "Okay, Simon out with it."

"Dad, I want to be a partner in the business, an equal fifty-fifty split the profits partner, and not a wannabe corporate partner like Christa was."

"You what!"

"I'm sure you heard me. Since he's dead — and I made that happen — he can't copy your system or sue you for vaporizing his company. I've earned my share. He was really smart, Dad. He figured out how to download the new operating system. And if he didn't get it, he was going public with a lawsuit to screw up your deal with Phillips, but then he went psycho. He killed Christa and tried to kill me."

"Simon, what the hell are you talking about?"

"You stole DataThink from him. I have the proof of what you did on his computer. And nobody knows about it but us. That's why you use DataThink as your password. Now do you remember him?"

Alex did remember months of threatening phone calls and e-mails that were silenced only by a Judge's restraining order. He was deeply shocked by his son's accusation and asserted, "My lawyer handled the takeover. I never met the man, and his name certainly wasn't Tim."

Simon shot back with surprising firmness that caused Alex's jaw to drop. "You stole from him. I couldn't believe you'd steal from anyone until I saw what he had on you in his computer."

Alex stood and demanded, "Why are you doing this to me?"

"To keep you honest. Now I want half of Greenlee or I go public."

"You wouldn't dare. You're only eleven years old."

"I'll soon be twelve."

When he saw the determined look on Simon's face, Alex knew he'd been cornered, "Alright, Simon. What else?"

"When our lawyer gets back tomorrow he can draw up the agreement. And I want Belle taken care of — Social Security, citizenship, health insurance, a retirement plan — the whole works. And equally important, Dad. We going to abandon that satellite umbrella link to a global mainframe. No amount of money is worth taking away what little freedom we have left. And I won't compromise on that."

"How did you learn to be so tough?"

"From Tim. And you."

The boy extended his hand and offered, "Deal?"

Alex looked down at Simon. He was proud of his son's toughness and smiled, "Okay, we've got a deal."

On the run back to the dock Alex shut down the skiff's outboard and they drifted amid the thick kelp beds watching the playful otters. Neither father nor son felt like talking. Then Alex felt Simon tense and saw him point to the outer edge of the kelp. Karl Mannheim was rowing his weathered dory in their direction. Simon was immensely relived that the old man was alive and apparently well. He waved at Karl, "Where have you been?"

"Fishing"

As the old Finn came closer Simon and Alex saw there was a line running from the dory's stern towing something large. After a few strokes more they could make out Tim's shredded body floating face up. Karl stood and calmly called across the water, "Hooked a big one, Mister Greenlee."

Simon had seen the bluish gray sheen of death by drowning once before. There was no possibility Tim, or whoever he was, could be alive. Simon was so relieved he began to collapse. Alex caught him and hugged his son tightly, "It's over now, Simon."

ACKNOWLEDGMENTS

Many thanks to Laird Koenig who helped frame the story and encouraged me to finish CA@UGHT IN THE WEB. David Konig, President of Editions Yago, Paris, first published the book as TR@HISON and arranged for Laurie Thinot's strikingly arresting cover. Christophe Rossen's insightful translation brought the characters to life. You three have made me proud.

This English edition has been expanded and enriched thanks to helpful suggestions offered by Al Zuckerman and his able assistant Mickey Leven. Sally Dalrymple, librarian, in Gisborne, New Zealand, reviewed the manuscript and offered valuable suggestions.

Special appreciation to Carl Hockey for sharing some gory video games with this writer. Thanks to fellow writer Susan Dworski for persistent encouragement. Son Pahl helped edit and the story was fulfilled. Thank you Sarah Dixon for skillful editing and typesetting.

Peter Dixon, Malibu, California

ABOUT THE AUTHOR

Born in New York City, Peter Dixon was a bi-coastal kid as his father, a writer, and his actor mother shuttled between New York and Los Angeles. His love for the ocean is a natural result of beginning to surf when he was in high school, lifeguarding on Los Angeles beaches through graduate school, and beach life in Malibu, California, with his wife, Sarah, and their three children.

Finding a career as a human factors scientist in a Santa Monica, California, "think tank" not to his taste, he turned to writing. The Complete Book of Surfing was the first widely read book on that wet and wild sport. He wrote the first Flipper television script, and several others for the series, followed by dozens of prime time teleplays while turning out twenty-nine published books. His recent novel Hunting the Dragon reflects his deep involvement with the sea and marine conservation.

Attention, Les Enfants Regardent, The Children Are Watching, written with Laird Koenig, was translated into seven languages, and was awarded best thriller of the year in France. Alain Delon produced and starred in the motion picture.

C@UGHT IN THE WEB brings to life Dixon's concern that TV and the Internet, while offering much of value, are also often a destructive force in the lives of children. He asks, if parents fail to open a child's life to the wider world of nature how will they learn to care for our earth and have compassion for one another?